*The Bla(

'Embodies an energy that is g

'An elemental book because the primitive passions run free.'
AE

Famine

'A major achievement – a masterpiece. The kind of truth only a major writer of fiction is capable of portraying.'
Anthony Burgess

'The author's skill as a storyteller is at times breathtaking. This is a most rewarding novel.'
Publishers Weekly

'A marvellously visual writer who prints his descriptions on the retina.'
The Guardian

Skerrett

'One of the most powerful novels that this master-writer has ever produced.'
Irish Times

'Liam O'Flaherty is a great, great writer whose work must be unique in any language, any culture. He has all the potential for becoming a matrix for the yearnings of another generation.'
Neil Jordan

'Powerful in language, majestic in scope, utterly honest.'
Sunday Press

Short Stories: The Pedlar's Revenge

'This valuable collection displays O'Flaherty's amazing range from a love idyll between a wild drake and a domestic duck to the unspeakable comedy of the appalling Patsa, from the burning of young love in that splendid story "The Caress" to the old love of "Lovers".'

Benedict Kiely

'This collection is a gallery of human emotions, embracing a clutch of huge eccentrics, sweet and sour remembrances of distant youth and vivid portraits of rural Ireland ... a worthy representation of an unflinchingly lyric writer.'

The Sunday Times

The Wilderness

'*The Wilderness* is essentially a simple story of unbridled passions, frustrated ambitions and hunger for land, but in the hands of O'Flaherty it becomes a *tour de force* that tears through the mind with the careless abandon of an Atlantic breaker.'

Sunday Press

LIAM O'FLAHERTY

Born in 1896 on Inishmore, the largest of the Aran Islands, Liam O'Flaherty grew up in a world of awesome beauty, echoes from his descendants and the ancient pagan past. From his father, a Fenian, O'Flaherty inherited a rebellious streak; from his mother, a noted *seanchaí* (storyteller), came the deep spiritualism and love of nature that has enraptured readers through the decades.

In France in 1917 O'Flaherty was severely shell-shocked. After a short recuperation, he spent several restless years travelling the globe. In 1920 he supported the Republican cause against the Free State government. Influenced by the Industrial Workers of the World's programme of social revolution, O'Flaherty organised the seizure and occupation of the Rotunda Theatre at the top of Dublin's O'Connell Street in 1922. He hoisted the red flag of revolution, calling himself the 'Chairman of the Council of the Unemployed', but fled three days later to avoid bloodshed. Later that year he moved to London, where his writing skills came to the attention of critic Edward Garnett, who recommended to Jonathan Cape the publication of O'Flaherty's first novel. For the next two decades, O'Flaherty's creative output was astonishing. Writing in English and Irish, he produced novels, memoirs and short stories by the dozen. Remarkable for their literary value and entertainment, O'Flaherty's books are also crucial from an anthropological point of view, charting the ways and beliefs of a peasant world before it was eclipsed by modernity.

Some of O'Flaherty's work was banned in Ireland – he was a rebel in his writing, as in his life. Liam O'Flaherty died in Dublin in 1984, aged 88 years, having enriched forever Irish literature and culture.

To Edward Garnett

LIAM O'FLAHERTY

the black soul

WOLFHOUND PRESS

First paperback edition, 1996
WOLFHOUND PRESS Ltd
68 Mountjoy Square
Dublin 1

and Wolfhound Press (UK)
18 Coleswood Rd
Harpenden
Herts AL5 1EQ

British Library Cataloguing in Publication Data
A catalogue record for this book is available from the British Library.

Wolfhound Press receives financial assistance from the Arts Council/
An Chomhairle Ealaíonn, Dublin.

ISBN 0 86327 478 1 paperback
ISBN 0 905473 63 9 hardback

Typesetting: Wolfhound Press
Cover illustration and design: Jon Berkeley
Printed in the UK by Cox & Wyman Ltd., Reading, Berks.

Winter

1

IN winter all things die. So roared the sea around the shores of Inverara. To the west beyond Rooruck it was black with dim fountains of white foam rising here and there as a wave formed and came towering to the beach. To the north, between Inverara and the mainland, it was white, like the waters of a mountain torrent, white with wide strips of green as if it had got sick and vomited. To the south it was black with a belt of white along the shore beneath the cliffs, where the breakers lashed the rocks. To the east beyond Kilmillick, where the north and south met in the narrow channel athwart the Head of Crom, it was a seething cauldron, hissing like a wounded snake. And around Rooruck it roared in mad delight.

Winter had come. The sea was wrecking all that had generated in spring, flowered in summer and borne fruit in autumn. It tore huge rocks from its bosom and sent them rumbling through the deep. It hurled weeds shorewards in a tumbling mass. They lined the beaches in mounds mixed with sand and the carcases of dogfish. It struck the cliffs monstrous blows that shook them and sent the rockbirds screaming from their clefts. They soared wildly out, their eyes searching the foam for fish.

In winter all things die. So shrieked the wind coming over the sea from the west. It rose from the sea and whirled upwards over the land. It mounted the wall of boulders that protected Rooruck on the west. It skirted the Hill of Fate that guarded Rooruck on the south. It swept eastwards, flying straight in its fury between earth and sky, blasting the earth. The grass was plucked up by the roots. Sheep fled bleating, seeking shelter among the crags. Horses neighed and ran in terror, their nostrils red. The goats wandering on the cliffs snorted and ran eastwards to the hollow beyond Coillnamhan. The fowls in the crops cackled and hid their heads among their feathers. Dogs howled. Pigs grunted and then huddled close together in their straw, whining. Old men sitting by the fires in their cabins shivered and felt that their death was near.

In winter all things die. The rain carried on the wind fell in great black drops that pattered on the crags and rose again in a blue mist. It came from the darkened sky sparse and scattered as if the clouds had been disembowelled in mid-air and only fragments of them had reached the earth terrified. There was no moon. It was hidden by the torn clouds. And the stars shone dimly in twos and threes, scattered over the firmament.

Between two hills, sheltered from the wind and from the sea, lay the seventeen cabins of Rooruck. Their thatched roofs, bound with thick ropes and laden with rocks, shivered but remained intact. The whitewash on their stone walls was blackened. Their doors were buttressed with stones and strips of sacking. Boards nailed into the wooden frames covered the windows. Here and there men stood at their gables leaning against the wind, their legs wide apart, their red lips opened outwards, their yellow teeth bared, their oilskin hats bound around their heads with strings. They shouted to one another from long distances, talking of the storm. Then they would shrug their shoulders, look at their thatch, and go indoors to their fires. Women with their red petticoats thrown over their heads hurried to the well for water. They stopped for a moment with their arms akimbo and their heads bent sideways close together, like birds, talking in awe of the storm and praising God who had not already destroyed them. Then night advanced and the hamlet was still, but for the barking of the frightened dogs.

At the most western point of the hamlet, nearest the shore and the sea, Red John's cabin lay huddled against the bluff of the hill. Around it the wind only sighed and moaned, for none but stray blasts reached it, blasts that had wandered from the storm, fallen in weariness from the whirling coils that rushed eastwards without pausing for breath. But the sea-spray sometimes struck the door, with a slow falling swish, as of a mountain of loose silk being crushed. The cries of the sea-birds that whirled about it sounded dismally. It was as if the lid were wrenched from the mouth of hell and the wailing of the damned came floating up from the distant caverns. But within there was warmth and peace, heightened by the storm without. In the kitchen a paraffin lamp burned dimly on the wall, its flame smoked with the draught that struck it from the chimney, discolouring the whitewashed wall behind it. On the open hearth a great turf fire burned, fanned by the draught. Its blaze was brighter than the lamp. Sometimes a blue snaky column shot up to lick the soot, that withered before it. The delf on the dresser gleamed in the half-light. Among the sooty rafters, where the earthen covering beneath the thatch hung down in dried lumps, there was darkness. And in the corners shadows seemed to lurk.

Red John sat on a three-legged stool in a corner to the left of the hearth, lighting his clay pipe with a coal that he had taken from the fire in a tongs. His red sunburned cheeks, seen through his red beard, were puffing in and out like a bellows as he sucked at the pipe. Then he dropped the coal into the fire and hit the dog that lay beside him on the hearth with the tongs. The dog whined and looked at him. But presently he sidled up again and stuck his nose in the yellow ashes. He sighed, and the outrush of his breath blew the ashes up on the legs of Red John's trousers. Red John cursed and struck the dog on the side with his rawhide shoe. The dog yelped and went to the dresser in two bounds. There he curled up and dug his snout into the spot where he had been kicked as if he had a flea, while his little eyes looked at Red John viciously.

Red John's wife sitting in the opposite corner looked at her husband and curled up her lips. Then she turned to the dog, cracked her fingers and said 'Poor doggie.' She did not feel compassion for the cur which she often beat herself, for it was a mangy mongrel. But she favoured it because her husband had kicked it. The cur rose and crept over to her almost on his belly, looking sideways at Red John. He lay by her lap wagging his tail and whining.

'Huh!' said Red John as he struck the turf fire with his shoe. His lips opened again to speak, and the tendons of his fingers rose in ridges on the back of his hands as if he were about to strangle his wife, but he neither spoke nor moved. He was afraid to strangle her, afraid even to speak to her. They hardly ever spoke during the five years they were married. And when they spoke, they spoke in hissing monosyllables. Sometimes they sat a whole winter's evening in silence, peering into the blaze. They hated one another. Red John, crabbit, weak-featured and bandy-legged, hated and feared Little Mary his wife; and Little Mary (so called because she was the tallest woman in Inverara) hated her husband and despised him.

Little Mary looked at her husband again, curled up her lips and opened wide her nostrils.

'Fcha,' she hissed, her hate boiling within her. She hit the dog and sent him away from her to the dresser, and gathering her black cotton shawl around her well-moulded breasts she looked into the fire, thinking.

'What is she thinking of now, the sorceress?' muttered Red John to himself. She was always thinking that way, sometimes showing her white teeth in a smile. That is why he feared her so. One could never know what was passing behind her high forehead. Red John huddled himself down to his knees and brooded on his folly in marrying her. Was she not the illegitimate daughter of Sir Henry Blake's housekeeper, of Blake Castle on the mainland? And the housekeeper herself was the illegitimate daughter of a Breton smuggler. The peasants knew it too, and often twitted him with taking a bastard woman to wife, one, too, with Blake blood in her. Often, when he was drinking in Mulligan's shebeen in Kilmurrage, a man would whisper in his ear, 'Is it true that woman of yours has dirty Blake blood in her, Red John?' Then Red John would pull off his blue woollen shirt and dance around the tavern floor, offering to fight the whole of Inverara, spitting on his hands between oaths. But he was so weak and inconsequent that everybody laughed at him. Even the small boys, when he passed them on his shaggy red mountain pony, shouted after him 'Empty Breeks,' the deadliest insult to a man in Inverara, where to be childless was to be impotent.

He peered across over his red beard at his wife's bosom. The right side of his face distorted, and his right hand shot into the pocket of his waistcoat for his knife. He longed to drive a knife down to the hilt in that breast. He often pictured to himself that thrust and the upward gush of red blood. He would lick his lips as if he were drinking it. But he was afraid. He was afraid. He, deformed himself, was afraid of touching such a beautiful thing, such well-moulded breasts, and red cheeks, and a neck like clear foam, and grey eyes that were always looking long distances, and black hair, straight black, rolled in a huge pile on her head. She was so different from any other woman in Inverara. 'Curse the night I went to Ballycalla,' he muttered. He had gone to the fair at Ballycalla on the mainland with his uncle, Sean Mor of Coillnamhan, and Michael the Drake of Kilmillick. Little Mary's mother was then living among the peasants after Sir Henry's death in France and the sale of his property, and they persuaded Red John to ask her for her daughter's hand in marriage. 'Curse the lips that said "yes," ' he muttered; 'don't make your house on a hill; don't marry a beautiful woman; don't ... don't ... don't ... may the devil mince her bones.' He was thinking of the wedding night. All the guests had departed drunk and singing, and he had tried to embrace her, but she hit him on the forehead a blow that sent him reeling against the kitchen wall. Then she went to bed alone, forcing him to sleep on a pallet in a corner of the room. And in all the five years he had never possessed her.

'Huh,' he cried, gathering fury, as he recalled the whole weight of his contumely. 'What are you sitting there for like a dead one? Why can't you speak to a man?'

Little Mary smiled scornfully without replying. Then she raised the hem of her red petticoat to allow the flames to warm her shins, or perhaps with feminine spite to madden her husband's lust with the sight of her well-shaped calves.

'You're not a man,' she said carelessly with a contemptuous shrug of her shoulders.

Red John fumed and chattered impotently.

She bared her white teeth, threw back her head slightly, nearly closed her eyes until the tips of the long lashes almost touched her cheekbones.

'Um-m-m-m,' she said.

Thousands of little snakes chased up and down her full white throat. Then her lips closed over her teeth and, opening wide her eyes, she looked again into the fire, thinking.

Men, men, men. How she wanted men, never having had any but this miserable lout of a husband, already beyond his youth when he married her, and never

shapely. The blood of her father, Blake, the aristocratic
gallant, and of her adventurous, fierce grandfather, Le
Cachet, made it impossible for her to love a peasant
like her husband, or any of the peasants she saw
around her in Inverara. They were too coarse. They
drank whisky to arouse their passion, and then mated
like pigs in their drunkenness. And the longing for
love burned as fiercely within her during those five
years that it broke through everything, shame, fear,
modesty. So when a painter had come from the
mainland to paint the breakers beneath the Hill of Fate,
she had smiled at him. She was gathering seaweed on
the shore with her husband when she saw him sitting
on a rock with his easel. She went up to him silently
and looked over his shoulder. Then she laughed. 'Paint
me too,' she cried, 'I am more beautiful than the sea!'
But he was a stupid Catholic and fled from her. And
then, unable to find love, she longed for a son. She
would sit by the fire and imagine that a son was
drinking at her breast. It soothed the aching within her.
She actually felt the impress of his toothless gums on
her nipples. And the blood would course madly up her
neck, swelling the veins as she shivered with passion.
Often she rushed from the cabin on a summer evening,
her bodice open at the neck, her light shawl across her
shoulders, seeking love, but the young men who
smiled at her when they met her repelled her. They
were yokels like her husband. There was a salt smell
from their bodies and their breath was fetid. Even
Father S – , who tried to touch her shoulder once in the
confessional, with the queer light in his eyes that all
men had when they looked at her, repelled her. He was
not a yokel, but . . . Ah! she wanted a fierce man and ...

A great wave rolled to the beach at the rear. Its wash sent a shower of water flying against the cabin. It fell with a great noise against the door, and the cabin shook slightly. Then a great falling sound came like thunder, followed by a tinkling reverberation like silver coin dancing on a plate: another rock had been torn by the sea from the Hill of Fate. Red John started and rose to his feet.

'The cabin will be swept away before morning,' he said.

Little Mary shrugged her shoulders. She did not care. Then Red John went to the door and opened it, and she saw the pitch darkness all around. A blast of wind rushed in with a querulous shriek, spilt a jug of milk on the dresser, and then died with a gasp as the door shut. She started and, bending her neck backwards, listened to the steady roar outside, the sea, the wind, the dogs, the birds, the falling walls, the driven rain.

Red John was bolting the door. 'He is out in that storm,' thought Little Mary. Then she peered at the chimney, her eyes gleaming, the tip of her tongue licking her lower lip. Her bosom and neck heaved as if somebody were trying to choke her. The hardness left her face, as if she were eager to be choked. She was thinking now of the man who had been in the cabin for the last seven days. That night week he had come with her husband from Kilmurrage. 'I want to be left alone,' he said, as he threw two suitcases on the kitchen floor. Great God, what a man he was! They said that the doctors had told him to come to Inverara as a cure for his nerves. He had been in the wars. At least so the people said. He had never spoken to her yet, or even looked at her except as an automaton who served his meals and made his bed. Everybody called him the 'Stranger,' but Seameen Derrane's daughter, who worked in Shaughnessy's hotel in Kilmurrage, where he had stayed the first three days after his arrival in Inverara, said that his name was Fergus O'Connor, and that he belonged to Ashcragh on the mainland, the little town south of the Head of Crom. They said too that he was mad, and had no religion. But she did not care what they said. He was the kind of man she wanted. His great black eyes pierced her like a wolfhound's, when he bent his forehead into furrows and his eyebrows contracted. And what a mouth he had! O God of the thousand battles, it was the kind of mouth she had kissed in her dreams, kissed until her lips were bruised. Long straight quivering lips! Of course he was thin and haggard, but all men were thin and haggard who lived hard. Why should men not live hard? Her own people had always lived hard. Her father had lived hard. Was not her grandfather, Le Cachet the Breton, shot during a drunken orgy in a brothel in the South of France? All real men lived hard, not slothfully, like pigs, as her husband lived, but wildly, like the storm that has no morals and recognizes no laws, but ruthlessly rushes forward and yet is beautiful in its ferocity.

Once she had touched his right hand below the wrist while handing him a cup of tea, and ... Virgin Mary, what a sensation! She had to turn away her head to hide her blushes. Would he never notice her? Perhaps he despised her as a peasant. Of course he was different. His hands were smooth and refined, and his face, in spite of the brown beard he was growing, was like her father's face. It had that peculiar expression in it that peasants did not have, as if it were concealing something. 'I will make him look at me,' she panted. 'There will be wreckage to-night,' said Red John, jumping to his feet. 'Get me my things ready. Sean Mor said he would come for me to go to the shore. Get my things, I say, woman,' he shouted, stamping on the floor.

She rose without speaking. It was as well to obey him. In Inverara all women obeyed their husbands, even though they hated and despised them. It was a custom, and customs are stronger than desires. She took a pair of old patched frieze trousers from a nail on the back door and threw them in the centre of the floor. On top of them she threw a heavy blue frieze shirt, an oilskin hat, a pair of raw-hide shoes, a waistcoat, a pair of woollen socks and a red muffler. She put half an oaten loaf in a handkerchief. She made tea and put it in a tin can. She tied a flannel cloth around the can to keep it warm. Then she sat again by the fire.

Red John took the clothes and went into the room on the right to dress himself. Little Mary was listening now for the sounds of footsteps. She was expecting the Stranger to come in any moment. How delicious it was to be expecting him. And she would be alone with him to-night while her husband was away. She started as a loud knock came to the door. She jumped up eagerly and unbarred it. But it was only Sean Mor, her husband's uncle. The great bulk of the fisherman stalked into the middle of the kitchen, shaking the rain from his clothes and stamping on the floor, crying that it was the worst night for forty years. He shuffled to a stool by the fire, leaving wet footprints on the earthen floor. Then he began to talk in a loud voice to his nephew who was still in the room.

Little Mary sat by the fire again. She knew Sean Mor was looking at her with his mind as he talked with his lips, leering with those small eyes of his. He was fifty, but strong and hardy, living on the sea, and his wife was a thin consumptive woman. Once he had tried to seize Little Mary, crying with a coarse guffaw, 'Now, if it were I who were living with you, there would be little voices in the house.' How hateful he was, with the tobacco stains on his beard and the black dirt beneath his gnarled nails.

'Well,' said Red John, coming from the room and taking his can of tea, 'in the Name of God, let us go.' They sprinkled holy water on themselves and said 'In the Name of the Father' as they crossed their breasts. The rain swept sideways into the kitchen as they went. Then the door banged, the lamp flickered, and there was silence. The dog smelt the door and then curled up by the fire on Red John's stool.

Little Mary was excited now. She was constantly shivering. Her passion surged up into her throat. She tripped around tidying the kitchen, her hips swaying like a dancer's. She combed her long black hair and put a ribbon in it. She turned around and around in front of the mirror by the lamp. She fidgeted, standing in front of the fire. She blushed as she toyed with the breast of her bodice. Then she gasped and put her hands to her heart as she heard footsteps coming around the gable-end. She had opened the door before the knock came.

As the Stranger entered, he stumbled against her, buffeted by the storm. 'I beg your pardon,' he said gently, and half-turned to her before he stopped short as if he remembered that he had committed an indecency, and his face set again in a scowl. Little Mary curtsied and smiled.

The Stranger went to the centre of the room and commenced to take off his dripping oilskin coat. Little Mary paused, half-ashamed to help him until he called sharply, 'Come, give me a hand, please.' As his face turned to her in the half-light, she could see that he was intoxicated, but she was not afraid of that. It seemed to her to be natural that her man should drink. Drink made men wild, and wildness was of the sea and of all things that were passionate and strong and beautiful. She took the coat gently from his shoulders and hung it on a nail. The Stranger, muttering something, kicked a stool to the front of the fire, sat down with a thud and spread his hands to the blaze.

'Will you have your supper now?' she asked.

He looked around at her contemptuously. 'Supper?' he said. 'Oh yes. Why not? I'm not hungry. Yes, of course I will.'

As she passed him going to and from the fire preparing supper, she kept looking at him, eager to speak and unable to begin. She was hoping that he would begin. After that it would be easy. But the Stranger kept silent. He had drunk several glasses of whisky in Derrane's shebeen, and the whisky had made him gloomy and depressed, as it always does with men whose souls are troubled. He kept looking into the fire, furrowing his forehead, twitching his nostrils and cracking the fingers of his right hand restlessly. His face, lit up by the firelight, was as pale as the face of a corpse, and the high cheekbones seemed to be straining against the skin like the ribs of an old cab-horse. His spine was distinct through the back of his coat as he sat leaning forward from the hips. But his eyes were wild and fierce. They would have kept a strong man away in fear from the wrecked body that encompassed them. They stared intently, and the lashes never blinked over them. But the brows kept contracting.

He sat trying to think, but the whisky made thought incoherent and illusory. The whining of the wind seemed to enter his brain.

'Are there eggs for me, Mary?' he said with a start, eager to busy himself with the world about him to prevent the mad rush of past memories that he felt were coming. They always came when he sat thinking.

'Yes, there are.'

'Oh, well, I don't want them.'

'But you must eat,' said Little Mary. 'A person must eat to live in this weather.'

He looked at her, about to argue with her, but he remembered that she was a peasant. She would not understand. He laughed and looked at the fire again. 'All right, Mary, I'll eat them.' Of course it would be ridiculous to talk to her. What in the name of the devil did she know about life? And why should he want to talk to people about important things, about life? He had come to Inverara to get rid of important things, of life. But was life important?

He clenched his hands and gritted his teeth to kill those hateful thoughts that began to rush into his mind like a shower of bullets fired in rapid succession. He moved his stool back from the fire with a nervous gesture, but the draught between the chimney and the door caught him, and he moved up again with a muttered oath. He began to tremble with rage. A dog began to bark in a cabin to the right. The roar of the sea became distinct and separate from the other sounds. He gasped and let his body go lax. He couldn't resist his thoughts. He couldn't govern them. With his lips wide open and a kind of wondering expression in his eyes he stared into the fire. Immediately something began to throb in his brain, like a motor, jumping back into the past. Then a door seemed to open – the door of his memory. It opened with a snap. As a whirlwind catches up suddenly a heap of snow, just around the bend of a mountain road, and lashes the countless flakes round and round in the air, the bulk remaining together in a winding column that rises higher and higher, while stray flakes drop from the white cloud, stand still for a moment and then fall into the valley beneath, so visions of his thirty years of life whirled round and round in the cell of his memory. One of them would break loose, pause for a moment at the door and then vanish. They did not come in the order of time or importance. They did not even seem to bear any relation to himself. In fact, he could see himself as if he were a stranger.

First he saw himself, a boy of twelve years, sitting in a brake with a score of other boys, some older than himself, some the same age. He was dressed in a knickerbocker suit with a belt down the back of the jacket, a school cap on his head, a cutaway starched collar over his jacket. Beside him sat a rosy-cheeked priest, with huge red hands, and his clerical waistcoat stained with snuff. The brake was approaching a large dome-shaped marble gate, with a large bronze cross

over it. All the boys were silent, some smoking
cigarettes. 'Ha, ha!' laughed the priest, 'this is the
Pearly Gate, my boys. No smoking allowed in Heaven.'
And as the brake scratched its way over the granite
dust in through the school-gate, the boys with a sigh
threw their cigarettes on the huge pile of other
cigarettes that lay to the left of the gate, under the niche
that held a statue of the Blessed Virgin.

That picture vanished. There was a hum in his ears,
and another picture stood out like a little red star. He
saw himself as an infant, sprawling naked in his
mother's lap. Black clouds were forming far away from
his eyes, and then they approached nearer and nearer
until they became little red spots. He was crying from
fear. He was afraid of his mother. He could see a queer
look in her eyes above him as he lay on his back. She
was fondling his naked toes, but she was laughing
boisterously at the same time and talking shortly to an
old woman who was mixing punch at the table. Then
that picture merged into another, in which he himself
did not figure. It was his home, a square grey building,
with a garden in front, white blinds drawn on the
upper windows, and the yellow chimney-pots
discoloured with black soot. Voices were coming from
the dining-room. His mother was shrieking, 'Oh then,
oh then, oh then! Are you going to murder me, John?
Can't I take a drop of brandy for my rheumatism? Oh
then, oh then, oh then!' Then his father came out and
banged the door behind him. He walked down the
gravel path to the gate, his left hand in his pocket, his
right hand stroking his brown beard, his grey cloth hat
pulled down over his eyes, a melancholy expression in
his face, his full red lips twitching. Next came a vision

of himself, at seventeen, standing over his mother's corpse. His father's hand was on his shoulder, the fingers clasping the shoulder-blade spasmodically. 'Fergus,' said his father, 'promise me now that you will never forget how . . .' And then the voice faded as he heard the parish priest denounce his father from the altar as an atheist, ordering his parishioners under pain of excommunication to keep their children from Mr. O'Connor's school.

'I should love to see that priest dying of cancer,' the Stranger muttered aloud.

Then came his father's death. It was a back room, in one of those drab streets off the South Circular Road in Dublin. He himself, then an enthusiastic youth of twenty, a brilliant student at the University, chaste, studious, supporting his father by clerical work in the evening in a newspaper office, while he maintained himself at college with scholarships, was holding his father's hand, comforting him, telling him he would be happy and prosperous yet. And the old man shook his head and said, 'I wonder, Fergus, is their hell as cruel as life?'

'Oh, damn it!' cried the Stranger, striking his forehead with his clenched fist.

Little Mary started and looked at him tenderly.

'Keep away from the fire,' she said, 'until you have eaten your supper. Food will settle your stomach. The heat goes badly with whisky.'

Ha! Now the visions became more comfortable. He could recognize himself as he was now. He was alone in the world, scoffing at the world. There was his first night at a music-hall. What a strange effect that had on him! When he saw the women, half-naked, displaying their plump limbs sensuously as they glided up and down the stage, he almost went mad with suppressed passion. He was then twenty-one and had never touched drink or knew women. That night after the theatre he tasted both.

'Of course. Why not?' he said aloud.

'What's that?' said Little Mary, as she laid a cup and saucer on the table.

'Oh, nothing,' grumbled the Stranger.

Little Mary shuddered and thought that it might have been the wind she heard. It sometimes seemed to talk with a human voice when it whistled around the western gable of the cabin, where the thatch rubbed between the two round stones that held the manilla ropes to the roof. Or it might have been the Wave of Destiny that roared distantly off the Fountain Hole. People said there was an underground palace there, submerged for thousands of years. Dead warriors feasted there in winter, and the sound of their banquet music was carried by the wind over the sea, to drive lonely women crazy with longing for love. She sighed and brushed the Stranger's elbow as she passed him to the fire.

The Stranger shivered inwardly as he felt her body touch his. He turned his head slowly to look at her. As she bent over the fire, with the fire-glow on her cheeks, she looked beautiful to him. But she did not arouse his passion. For him it was like looking at a statue.

'Women are a curse,' he muttered. 'No, no. Not a curse, but the playthings of folly, disused. ....'

With a snap the motor in his brain began to purr again. Again a picture eddied out of the mass of memories and stood still. It was the picture of the night with his first woman. She became distinct for a moment, beautiful eyes burning like coals in the wreck of a beautiful face, a loose soiled dressing-gown with a fleshless collar-bone showing at the open neck. Then the woman vanished as she held out her thin hands and said, 'Are you leaving me so soon, dearie?' He himself became distinct, wandering through back streets, tearing his hair, cursing himself, feeling his body unclean, begging the earth to open up and devour him. Then a whole series of pictures came with a rush, crowding one over the other. That was his year of debauch before he joined the army. At last the pictures joined together and formed into one. He saw himself standing outside a recruiting office, down at heel, in a tattered coat, with sunken cheeks. Then a monstrous picture came, distorted like a madman's fancy. It was a vast plain without a tree or a blade of grass, pock-marked with shell holes, covered with rotting corpses. He could see the vermin crawling on the dead lips. And he smiled. That picture did not accuse himself. It accused the world that he hated. 'Just think of it,' he muttered, 'I spent three years in that hell. Great God!'

He smiled as he saw himself wandering around the world for two years after the war, trying to find somewhere to rest – Canada, the Argentine, South Africa. 'What a blasted fool I was! As if there were any rest for a man in this world!' And then, worse still he saw himself back again in Dublin, burrowing in the bowels of philosophy, trying to find consolation one day in religion, next day in anarchism, next day in Communism, and rejecting everything as empty, false and valueless. And at last, despairing of life, flying

from it as from an ogre that was torturing him, he had
come to Inverara.

He jumped to his feet, and with his hands behind
his back he began to stalk up and down the floor,
muttering disjointedly:

'Honour, civilization ... eh ... all rot ... culture be
damned ... all the culture in the world ... prostitution
and hypocrisy ... only thing is to live like a beast
without thought ... not to give a damn . . .'

'Your supper is ready,' said Little Mary.

He had forgotten his supper, and he felt no desire to
eat. Still, he had no energy to refuse it. What did it
matter, anyway, he thought, whether he ate or did not
eat? 'In the world men make revolutions in order to
eat. How ridiculous!' He took a seat at the deal table.
He broke an egg and tasted it.

'Drink the tea first,' said Little Mary. 'It will do you
good.'

'Oh, for God's sake, woman, let me alone. How do
you know what's good or bad?'

Mary almost dropped the kettle she was taking from
the hearth. She whirled around like a tigress. Her eyes
blazed. He had sworn at her. Her lips went white. Her
husband had often sworn at her. The men around
Rooruck always swore at their women and often beat
them. But she had expected that this man would have
been refined. He had insulted her! She forgot that she
was a peasant. Her father's blood boiled in her. The
hand holding the kettle shivered. Then her anger fled
in a flash. Instead she felt a throbbing of her breast. It
hurt her, as fire hurts a numbed hand. The Stranger
had looked at her fiercely, and before his stare her
anger had changed into the hunger of love. She felt a

physical pain as if he had beaten her with a stick. It was more cruel than that. He had burnt her with his tongue and his eyes had drawn the sting from her body, leaving it numb. She sighed. Her breast heaved and her eyes dimmed with sadness looking into his. They said, 'Come, you may kill me. I am yours.'

He looked at her through the mist that the whisky raised before his eyes, and thought that she was a *cocotte* ogling him. He could see her only at a far distance. Between his eyes and hers there were a host of visions – his mother, his father, his youth that was pure, his debauched manhood, and the horrors of war. All these visions told him that she was a *cocotte*, 'like all women,' that she would look at all men as she looked at him. Beyond these visions was the beauty of her sad eyes and her swelling white throat. That beauty attracted him. But his soul, enraged with his sordid past, hissed at the beauty and scowled, persuading itself that the woman was repulsive, 'like all women.'

'I won't let the slut drag me back to life,' he muttered, savagely eating his griddle cake.

And Little Mary moved about the kitchen excitedly, watching him without looking at him.

'He has trouble on his mind,' she thought. 'I will wait. Wait, wait, wait for ever.'

The Stranger finished his meal and sat again in front of the fire. Little Mary cleared the table and sat in the corner beside him looking into the fire. And then he began to feel her presence drawing him towards her again. His mind was bored. It was his body that was excited. It was an ugly excitement that filled his mind with repulsion. He struggled against it, but it remained. Then he looked at her with the look in his eyes that all men had when they looked at her. She shuddered. The accumulated passion of years was burning in her and she was eager for his love. And yet she began to feel afraid. She did not see the light of love in his eyes. She wanted him for ever. And that hot passion in his face was like what she saw in all men's faces. It was lust. He had arisen from his stool and was moving slowly towards her, his hands shaking.

'No, no,' she cried with her lips, as her body moved towards his. 'No, no. I ... I ... don't.'

He swore as he grasped her shoulders, and then there was a loud roar that sent them both to their feet gasping.

The cabin shook. Thunder crashed across the heavens. The slits between the boards on the windows were bright with the forked lightning. The sound came rumbling from east to west louder and louder, as if each peal gave birth in its passage to a peal louder than itself. Through the sound of the thunder came the screech of the wind. And the sea roared monotonously like a hungry lion. The air was full of sound.

The Stranger stood transfixed by the fire. Little Mary stood beside him looking up at him, careless of the storm. Then she threw her arms around his neck and pressed close to him feigning fear.

'Protect me,' she murmured.

He thrust her gently from him and went to the centre of the floor, trembling. He felt that the thunder had clapped as a warning to him. It warned him against falling a victim to passion. So God might have warned a hermit monk of old. He became full of self-pity. He told himself that the whole world was in arms against him, dragging him back again into the torture from which he had fled. Even here, to the desolate bleak fastness of Rooruck, the wickedness of the world had pursued him. These passions and desires of the flesh were ugly and futile. Passion belonged to young men, full of the enthusiasm of youth. It belonged to the chattering mob. He was dead to it. He had heaped huge rocks on its grave.

'Ye-ah,' he said, baring his teeth. A demoniac look came into his eyes. Then his stomach turned. He went stumbling to the door and out into the night.

Little Mary dropped into her seat by the fire. Her bosom heaved with sobs. She bit her finger, trying to think what was the matter with her. Her body felt as if pins were being stuck through every pore of her skin. The soles of her feet itched. 'Virgin Mary,' she kept saying, 'what is coming over me? I love him, I love him.'

She could not look at him when he came in. She wanted to be alone with this wonderful thing that had seized her body. She wanted to master it.

He stood at the door dripping with rain, his black hair in a matted mass about his face. Nothing of his face was visible but his bloodshot black eyes staring wildly. His bosom heaved as he hiccupped. Then he stumbled to his room, tore off his clothes, and fell on the bed. In a moment he was fast asleep. His passion died and left him as helpless as death, for in winter all things die that live in summer.

But even in winter, morning brings life and motion. It is a glorious motion to the strong, that winter movement of life in Inverara. It makes the body feel clean and the mind strong, as if it were bound with laths of steel. But for the weak, of body or of mind, it is a torture. The sun rose in the east, dim and sour, with a veil over its face. It sank again in the west without warming the earth. The birds were silent, hiding in their holes, or fled to the mainland over the sea, sitting on the masts of ships, searching the south and the sun. The sea moved mightily. At times it rested, green and bilious, between two battles. And the wind whined when the sea was resting. Everywhere in Inverara there was death on the ground and above it. The people went about clad in their heavy frieze, talking in low voices. At night they sat in the shebeens and around their own hearths telling stories of wrecks and drowning and death. Even sin had fled, for sin is born of the languorous passion of summer, and of the cold gritty breezes of spring.

Little Mary, her soul strong like the fierce soul of winter, was happy. She had found a man to love. He had spurned her. What of it? So did the sea spurn in winter and caress in spring and love in summer. What of it? She sang as she milked her cow in the morning. She sang as she went to the village well for water. The peasant women noticed her joy and began to whisper among themselves and point fingers at her. 'O wife of Red John,' they would say to her, with mock anxiety and a vicious gleam in their eyes, 'what kind of man is he who is lodging in your house?' 'They say he is mad from the wars; beware of him,' whispered another. 'How handsome he is! Does he talk to you nicely?' whispered another. And they would all laugh. And Little Mary, careless of their chatter, would throw back her head and laugh, her throat swelling like the throat of a singing thrush. Her husband began to look fearfully at her and say to himself, 'What has come to the woman? Eh, Red John, what has come to her?'

To the Stranger those days were a torture. Afterwards they remained only as a blur on his memory, the blur that rises before the mind when the fumes of chloroform are sucked up the nostrils as if mountains were crowding up to crush one's life, with loud awe-inspiring sounds. In the morning he would walk up and down the crag overlooking the Hill of Fate. His figure stooped. His head was thrust forward between his shoulders. His lips were compressed. There was a scowl on his face that terrified people who saw him. Often the small boys of the village peeped at him through the holes in the stone fence that runs parallel to the cliff. But their mothers would drive them away saying, 'Lord have mercy on us. It's a curse is on his soul. Father Shannon, may God be good to the poor man, was the same way after they unfrocked him.'

Then another terrific night of storm came. A Norwegian barque was wrecked off the Head of Crom and all her crew were drowned. Sheep and goats were killed on the crags by the storm. The bleak morning saw the peasants of Rooruck quarrelling on the shore, up to their necks in the huge breakers, grabbing at the planks and spars of the wrecked ship. The Stranger watched them, horrified, watching the living looting the house of the dead. Then he strode eastward to the cliffs. The storm of the night still raged. The salt spray whirled past him, climbing the two hundred feet from the sea in one light leap. The thundering waves rolled beneath madly. They rolled gaily, advancing, retreating, rising and falling with the rhythm of an orchestra. He was seized with their madness. He walked up and down the cliff revelling in it. The sea and the wind were mad, and he felt that he too was mad with them. They were committing suicide in their madness. So would he. But as soon as the thought came it terrified him. When he looked down through the spray at the white foam on the dark heaving bellies of the sea, he thought they were grinning at him. And he fled back to the cabin.

He locked himself in his room all the day, lying on the bed on his back looking at the ceiling. Little Mary called him to his midday meal, but he growled at her to leave him alone. Then when darkness began to fall he left the house and went into Derrane's shebeen at the eastern end of the village. Derrane's kitchen was empty that night. All the people were at the shore salving the wreck of the Norwegian ship. He sat in a corner by the fire drinking glass after glass of potheen. Derrane's wife, an inquisitive, loose-tongued woman, tried to draw him into conversation, asking him what did he think of the women of Rooruck. He did not reply, but she kept on talking after the manner of women.

At last she was saying, 'And sure it's the hand of God . . .' when the Stranger flung his glass into the fire and jumped to his feet.

'May the devil devour both you and God,' he yelled, frothing with rage. The woman screamed, and he danced around the room shouting, 'Yes, to hell with God. To hell with Him, I say. What do you know about the fool?' Then he rushed out of the house and staggered up the boreen to Red John's, shouting. Little Mary came running down to meet him and dragged him indoors.

A group of women gathered outside the gate of Red John's yard listening to the sounds of quarrelling that came from the house.

'Lord save us, it's murder,' said one.

'Let somebody go to the shore for the men,' said another.

Then Red John came rushing from the cabin, his forehead bleeding from a long cut that reached from the right eye to the right temple. The women shrieked and crowded about him.

'What has come to you?' they gasped.

Red John stood for a few moments spluttering and waving his hands in the air.

'Police, police,' he yelled. 'The son of misfortune came in blaspheming and I tried to send him from the house and the loose woman on whom I put a ring gave me this. Police, police.' And he rushed away for his pony. He rode madly into Kilmurrage for the police, but passing the schoolmaster's house he got afraid. He dismounted from his pony and let it wander home alone. Then he went across the crags to Branigan's shebeen in Kilmillick. He spent the night there drinking. The first streaks of the grey dawn were beginning to light the crags about Rooruck when he crept into his cabin and sat by his bed, shivering. He could hear his wife crooning in the Stranger's room, as if she were rocking a child.

'Ho-wa, ho-wa my pulse, white love of my heart. Ho-wa, ho-wa, brilliant gem of gladness. Ho-wa.'

He listened with open mouth.

'Ha,' he said fearfully, his hand on the white bandage that covered his wound, 'he has put a spell on her. So he has.' Hurriedly he put an oaten loaf in a cloth and left the cabin to look for wreckage.

The Stranger slept through the day. It was his first refreshing sleep since he had come to Inverara. Little Mary moved noiselessly about the cabin. Now and again she stood at her cabin door and looked longingly out towards the mainland. She could see it distantly when the mist broke, scattered by the breezes that blew intermittently over the green sea. She would go into the darkened room where he lay and look at his face, gentle and childish in sleep. Once she bent down and caressed his hair and his forehead with her lips.

The Stranger, sleeping, dreamt that a fairy had touched him. He kept dreaming a long time of beautiful women, with roses entwined in their black hair, kissing his lips. Then he awoke and saw only a peasant woman standing by his bed. The consciousness of his degradation swept back to him. He swallowed a cup of hot tea, dressed and went out. Night was falling in a thick mist that coloured everything pale blue. He felt a dryness in his throat.

'Hell,' he said, 'I must get somebody to talk to. It's awful being alone like this among yokels who only stare with open mouths when a man talks to them. I wish I hadn't come here.' But trudging along the wet road, the ends of his oilskin coat swishing damply against his legs, he shuddered as he thought of staying in Dublin 'among so many people that don't seem to care a damn.' He could see that evening he went to Dr. McCarthy and said that he couldn't sleep. 'Hey, my boy, can't sleep, eh?' cried McCarthy, his fat stomach puffing in and out as he paced up and down the

hearthrug. 'You say you are working in the library. Like
the work?' 'I hate it.' 'Any money left?' 'About two
hundred.' 'Well, get to blazes out of Dublin then. Go out
to the west and catch fish. Do you more good than
cataloguing books. Out with ye, as quick as lightning.'
The tramcars sounded in his ears that evening as he
rushed away from the doctor's as loud as an artillery
barrage. He hardly breathed peacefully until he left the
Broadstone Station next morning. And now ...

'Damned if I'm going back again,' he muttered.
'Some day I'm going to throw myself down from that
cliff and be done with it. By all the gods, I will. You see
if I don't.'

Then he heard the sounds of music as he was
approaching John Carmody's public-house at the
cross-roads above the beach at Coillnamhan. He
stopped dead in the road and listened.

Night had fallen. It was bitterly cold, but there was
no wind. The wind was drowned by the wet fog, that
came like a great blight from the mountains on the
mainland to the north. He could dimly see the lights of
the publichouse, a squat one-storied concrete building
on a slope a little back from the road. John Carmody
had built it the year before. It looked as incongruous in
the surroundings as the electric railways at Niagara
Falls. And the sounds of wild music came through its
windows. The music had a peculiar effect on the
Stranger. Music of any kind always maddened him
with a sad happy madness. It affected him in the
bowels. He often cried with the sadness of the thoughts
that it inspired within him. At other times it made him
want to kill. Now as he listened to the rough twanging

of the accordion he was wrapped in an ecstasy of sadness.

He walked up a bypath to the house over trodden grass, avoiding the road, lest he should lose the sound of the music. He tripped over an empty barrel and fell against the door. The music stopped suddenly. Somebody jumped to his feet within and shouted, 'God with you.' Then the door opened and he entered the kitchen.

The kitchen covered half the floor space of the house. To the right was a counter cut into the partition, and behind the partition was a room lined with shelves of black-brown bottles and green bottles. Several barrels were pushed back, their round heads over the counter. On the counter John Carmody was leaning smoking a pipe, while his wife wiped a pint mug behind him. Around the fire on the hearth and on wooden forms by the wall a number of peasants sat drinking and smoking. Two of them had been dancing when the Stranger entered. Another group had been listening to John Carmody discussing politics. For the good man, even though he was now nearing middle-age and had become, as he himself said, a 'bourgeois' (a word the peasants understood to mean 'an enemy of God'), he still liked to preach Socialism when he was in a good humour and slightly intoxicated.

'I'll make you fellahs drink out of a trough,' he would say, 'if you don't get busy and organize to socialize the land and industry, and do away with the priests.'

And the people just thought that he was a harmless poor man and well-meaning.

There was silence when the Stranger entered.

'Who is that fellah?' said John Carmody to a man who stood beside him.

The man bent his mouth close to Carmody's ear and whispered:

'That's Red John's lodger. They say he's gone in the head. We call him the Stranger.'

'Go away, you galoot,' said Carmody. 'I heard about him. If you fellahs were as cracked as he is you wouldn't be the bloody fools you are.'

He coughed loudly, stepped into the kitchen, and advanced to the Stranger who was sitting on a form by the back door.

'Say,' he cried in a loud hearty voice, 'I'm tickled to death to see a live man come into my house. Shake! Stranger. You must have a drink with me.'

As soon as the peasants saw Carmody welcoming the Stranger, they looked at one another and whispered: 'He must be all right after all.'

For Mrs. Derrane had broadcasted the story of the night before, and with the quickness of peasants to believe harm of everybody, no matter how ridiculous the story might be, they all thought the Stranger possessed of a devil. The music started once more and a ragged fisherman with a dirty black beard got up to dance a hornpipe. He did a few whirls clumsily, but he was so drunk that he stumbled straight backwards trying to clap his hands under the crook of his left knee, and fell on his buttocks in a pot at the back door.

'Oh, you God of all evil!' he cried mournfully, amid a roar of laughter.

The Stranger, sitting beside Carmody on the form, laughed as loudly as the rest. He felt a strange joy in

the association of these people. They appeared to him
to be real. He felt the joy that the bad young man feels
when he returns to the tavern after spending an
evening with genteel and boring society in the
respectability of his home. And he felt drawn towards
Carmody in particular. He drank the bad brandy that
was offered to him, and somehow it tasted better than
anything he had ever drunk. Carmody began to talk at
a great pace about the United States, where he had
spent ten years of his youth.

'A great country. None o'yer goddam superstitions
there.'

The Stranger felt a sense of freedom creeping over
him. The outspoken wanderer, Carmody was, he felt,
an outcast from society like himself, at war with the
world. He was a kindred spirit. 'Ha, ha,' he thought, it
would be a great life to lounge around in Inverara,
drinking and talking to Carmody, enjoying himself,
abandoning himself, without any thought of the world
outside, just living like a pig. It would be a revenge on
the world. It would be far better than to kill himself. If
he were dead he could not feel anything, whereas
alive, his life would be a constant insult to civilization.
Civilization? That cursed quagmire that sucked
everything good into its bosom! That mirage that lures
youth with promises that are never fulfilled! Sure. This
was the ideal thing. To meet a few fellows like
Carmody and drink with them and scoff at the world
with them, laughing loudly to cheat the blackness in
his soul. He would wear his body away until the damn
thing fell to pieces. He would use up every ounce of it
in wild debauch.

He felt himself getting drunk, and was glad. It was the first time he felt the exhilaration of drunkenness since he had come to Inverara. The whisky he had drunk in the shebeen only stupefied him. The company prevented him from getting drunk. Talking to a man like Carmody he could get drunk. He seized Carmody's hand. Carmody turned his long bronzed muscular face towards him.

'I'm glad I met you,' he said, 'I've been dying for somebody to whom I could talk.'

Carmody was about to reply when somebody stumbled against the barrel outside the door. There was a loud string of curses.

'Another man fallen,' shouted a peasant.

'Blast ye, Michaeleen Grealish,' shouted Carmody, 'didn't I tell ye to take away that - - - - barrel?'

'Hey there, hey there,' came the voice, 'open the door. I can't see my hand.'

Somebody raised the latch and a man flopped into the kitchen with his left hand held out in front of him. He began to talk as soon as he was within the house and he kept talking. His voice rang out loud and clear. He kept gesticulating with both hands and throwing his head back with a twist, like a dog shaking a rat. He had taken his hat from his head and his bald forehead shone in the light. The lumps on the white skin around the temples stood out distinctly. His grey bushy eyebrows twitched. His cheeks were blood red, with narrow blue veins showing through them. His nose was long and straight. Its ridge was as sharp as a lean horse's spine. He wore a bushy grey beard, shaven on both lips. His chin showed red through the beard, and it had a dimple in the centre. His blue eyes gleamed like the bright blue dust that shines in granite. His grey trousers hung close to his thin legs, showing the outward bend in the left leg below the knee. His black coat hung loose about his body.

'Somebody wants to kill me,' he cried, his blue eyes glaring all around him fiercely. Yet everybody laughed. Then the man opened his mouth too and laughed. He had only five teeth in his upper jaw, scattered at irregular intervals.

'Say, you must excuse me, Mr. O'Daly,' said Carmody, coming up to him. 'I told that fool Michaeleen –'

'That's all right, my good man, that's all right. Good evening,' he said, seeing the Stranger, 'I heard you were staying at Red John's. I meant to go and see you. Come on, look alive there, Carmody, and bring a bottle into the parlour. Bring a glass for yourself.'

'A bottle of that best brandy, Mary,' shouted Carmody to his wife as he respectfully went in front to open the parlour door. He placed chairs in front of the parlour fire and asked his guests to seat themselves, hitching his American trousers about his waist and spitting on his hands like a waiter in a New York bowery lunch room. His huge stature loomed over the two middle-sized men like the figure of a Praetorian guardsman protecting a Caesar.

'Let me introduce you –' he began.

'I always introduce myself,' interrupted O'Daly, leaning back with his two feet crossed on the mantelpiece until his chair stood on its hind legs. 'My name is Matthew O'Daly of Lisamuc, Co. Sligo.'

He threw out his chest as he spoke and his eyes flashed. He made a gesture with his left hand in front of his face and then rubbed it along his left shin as he turned to the Stranger, his eyes gleaming aggressively as if he were challenging the Stranger to doubt his identity. The wrist above his hand seemed to be made solely of a square flat bone, covered with white hairy skin. In fact, all his body seemed to be made of one flexible bone like a steel sword.

The Stranger winced, and blinked his eyes under the unexpected stare. It was some time before he could get himself to give his own name. Suddenly it occurred to him that he was ashamed of his name, of his ancestry, that his father was an obscure schoolmaster, that he himself was a failure in life and a coward.

'My name is Fergus O'Connor of Ashcragh,' he said with an affected drawl.

'Heh,' said O'Daly. Then he made a noise at the back of his palate like a man urging on a horse.

'I declare to Christ but you must be the son of John O'Connor the schoolmaster. Hell to my soul, that dog of a priest treated him badly. Shake hands.'

Carmody's face beamed at hearing O'Daly abuse a priest, and he hit himself a great blow in the chest and laughed until his teeth seemed about to fall out. He hated priests as enemies of 'all people who can think intelligent.'

'Drink up,' he said, handing them glasses from the tray that had been brought in. 'You two will drink on me to-night. It's seldom that three men –'

But O'Daly interrupted him again, and began to talk at a tremendous rate, denouncing the parish priest, the doctor, the district inspector of police, and all the people of note in Inverara, as scoundrels of the worst kind, inhuman rascals, low fellows, and men whose parentage was in doubt.

'Since this new Government came into power, Carmody,' he cried, 'the country is gone to the dogs.'

The Stranger drank his brandy and felt the blood rushing to his head. Suddenly he began to lose his grip of everything. He became defiant and aggressive. He joined in the conversation and began to boast on his own account, boasting of his past life, of which he had been mortally ashamed an hour ago. Carmody began to boast, but O'Daly boasted loudest of them all. None of the three would listen to the others. Only snatches of their conversation rose above the volume of sound, amid the clinking of glasses and the gurgling of the brandy from the bottle. It seemed that the three of them had spent all their lives fighting, drinking, and breaking women's hearts. O'Daly spent more nights of his sixty years of life in his boots than out of them. He had drunk more whisky 'than they make now in the distilleries.' He had broken a man's hand in two places with a simple twist of his wrist. He had been all over Ireland, and knew every bishop, politician, racehorse-owner and athlete. In other words, he knew every body whom anybody cares to be known to know in Ireland. Carmody was not behindhand. In fact, he had once stood, it seems, as a candidate for the American Congress in the Socialist interest. He was known all over the American continent as a crack shot, and he had more love affairs than he could count. The Stranger had been one of the most gifted and promising geniuses in Europe before the war, drink and women laid him low.

Then they became slightly maudlin. The Stranger felt that he was enjoying himself as he had never done before. He kept laughing boisterously for no reason in the world. He felt sure that he would live happily for ever in Inverara in this society. Suddenly death appeared to him to be a menace that he must avoid.

'Hey,' he hiccupped, leaning over to O'Daly, 'what do you think of the next world?'

O'Daly made a noise again like a man urging on a horse.

'Look here,' he said, 'it's only the young that can afford to waste their time thinking of the next world. As far as I know, this world is too short and it's seldom Carmody offers us free brandy. Drink to life and damn the next world. Let's have a song before we go.'

Hot and foolish with drink they began to sing some ridiculous thing out of tune. Before the first verse was finished, each was singing a different song. Then Carmody suddenly dropped his head on the table and fell asleep. O'Daly shook him and tried to wake him. Carmody raised his head and stuttered:

'Come in here every evening ... talk about Karl Marx.' Then he dropped asleep again.

'Hell to my soul,' said O'Daly, 'who is this fellow Marx he's always talking about? Must owe him some money. Tight-fisted fellows, these publicans, between the two of us. Come on up to my house and let him sleep.'

The two of them got into O'Daly's jaunting car that was waiting in the yard. The hardy mountain pony, careless of the freezing mist, had been contentedly chewing bad hay there for two or three hours. They drove up through the village at a walking pace. O'Daly explained that he had been into Kilmurrage to attend a meeting of the local court.

'This new Government made me a magistrate,' he shouted. Then he began again to denounce everybody, and the cruelty of bad fortune that had pursued him and his family for generations. He lashed the mare furiously as he spoke, but the mare's hide was obviously as tough as his own, and she never changed her gait. 'I have to live up here in a little cottage with my daughter and an old woman who looks after the place. She's even too old to sleep with. And my daughter has to teach these brats in the school for a living. Everybody has to work for a living nowadays. The world is changed. So it is. I remember in my time ... Begob, my daughter is a poor specimen of a woman compared to her mother. In my time they were as wild as the men, strong, hefty women. Ah well' ... And he went on to tell stories of his youth, and of the glory of his ancestors, stories which were for the most part lies, for the days when the O'Dalys of Lisamuc were people of importance were too distant to be remembered by anybody.

The cold mist was scattering the exhilarating effect of the brandy from the Stranger's mind. He began to be melancholic and dissatisfied again. He grew jealous of O'Daly's strength, of his coolness and strong nerves.

'Ah,' he said to himself, 'he has no intellect. That's what it is.' And he cursed God for having given himself a strong intellect until he remembered that there was no God and became still more depressed because he had nobody to blame for his sorrow. Then, in order to ease the pent-up volume of his sadness, he began to tell O'Daly his troubles, but O'Daly paid no attention to him. He continually interrupted with his own reminiscences.

'You're a young man,' he would say, 'and you don't understand the world. Now, in my time, the young men feared nothing. Not even the devil in hell. Is it that measly war you're talking about? Sure that was only a cockfight compared to what I've seen in my young days.'

They reached O'Daly's cottage. The Stranger, irritated because O'Daly would not pity him, wanted to go home immediately, but O'Daly would have none of it. He stood in the middle of the road, one hand holding the reins, the other hand grasping the Stranger's shoulder.

'See that house of mine,' he shouted at the top of his voice. 'There's a hovel for an O'Daly to live in! Hell to my soul, but the world is gone to the dogs. Listen to me' – he panted loudly and wheezed –'listen to me. The O'Malleys used to live here in the old days. And now where are they? Gone to hell. Gone and forgotten. There isn't a trace of them. The last of them, devil take him, he had queer notions in his head, I hear; ran away to America with a slip of a flighty woman. And there you are. Wait there till I put the mare in the stable.'

The Stranger stood leaning against the gate leading up to the cottage. He became ashamed of having been fond of life an hour before. He felt as a monk might feel after being seduced by a woman. Blackness gathered again around his soul. 'I made a fool of myself,' he muttered.

The mist seemed to stick like icicles to his cheekbones. He wanted to run away, but he hadn't the energy to make up his mind to do anything. His stomach became as hard as a ball. It robbed him of all energy. Weakness crept through the extremities of his hands and feet. Then O'Daly came along breathing loudly. The Stranger felt that he could kill the man for his very power to breathe so loudly.

'Come on in,' said O'Daly gruffly. 'Make as little noise as ye can,' he added. 'I don't want to wake Kathleen. The poor girl has to go to that damn school in the morning. The shame and disgrace of it is killing me.'

They crept on tiptoe up the path and into the kitchen by the back door. O'Daly was staggering a little. He lit a candle and placed it on a table in the centre of the room. Then he got a bottle from somewhere and two empty cups without handles. They set to drinking again. O'Daly became maudlin, crying about the fallen fortunes of his family. The Stranger suddenly became afraid, afraid of O'Daly, afraid of the dark kitchen with the dim flickering candle standing in the centre of it like a warning of death, afraid of the dark silent night outside, with the sound of the sea coming from a distance. He drank hurriedly, but the drink seemed to evaporate impotently in his throat. It tasted like water. Strange shadows began to gather before his eyes. He started at every sound. He couldn't see O'Daly, but he could hear his quavering voice. The sea rolling on to the beach at Coillnamhan reminded him of the 'keene' women at wakes over dead bodies. It was as if one heard a pot boiling a million miles away. And to the south against the cliffs it sounded like a great weight falling swiftly into a deep cavern. Then he jumped to his feet as he heard O'Daly snore.

He listened for a full minute, breathing gently, perfectly motionless. In that minute he felt that he was a pure soul being judged by wicked demons. Then his mouth gaped as the picture of the night he was buried by a shell in France flashed before his mind. A cormorant called dismally passing over the house. He listened to the swishing wings. Then his right knee began to tremble. His left foot began to tap the ground. He bent down carefully to hold it steady.

'Hold on there,' he muttered, trying to laugh.

Then his whole body trembled. Beads of cold sweat poured out through his forehead and neck. With an oath he shot out his hands and made for the door. He felt sure that he would be dead before he reached the open air. The round ball in his stomach was stifling him.

The night air revived him. He laughed at his fears. He straightened himself when he got into the road and said, 'Pooh, I'm all right.' But at that moment the wind rose suddenly. A squall came from the south over the crags. It came with a swoop. He gasped and his eyeballs started. As he ran headlong forward, fantastic visions crowded into his mind. He saw millions of dying men, worlds falling to pieces, continents being hurled into the air, while he himself wandered among the chaos, the only living atom in the wrecked universe. He ran faster, trying to escape the vision, but they pursued him, crowding on one another, cries of the wounded, shrieks of the damned, corpses piled mountain-high, races wandering across deserts, chasms opening everywhere, devils grinning, wild animals with gory jaws rushing hither and thither in dark forests, myriads of men talking in strange languages, gesticulating, shouting furiously, the wails of women, the bodies of children transfixed on spears.

Over all came the noise of the guns, millions of guns, rising and falling and intermingling. Their sound was like a millrace. It made beautiful music that enthralled him and made him want to kill. Then the music died and dread spectres returned. They were bare grinning skulls now and fetid smells. His body was rising into space and flying away, headed for the moon. But there was a great weight tied to the stomach that held it back. His brain began to expand. It covered the earth and then the universe, and then it burst, hurting his forehead.

He had fallen against the door of Red John's cabin. He was unconscious when Little Mary threw herself on his neck. Folly, folly, folly, what is folly?

2

At Rooruck winter sleeps in its depths. But it's a troubled sleep, sad, weary, and full of nightmares. It is the sleep of a wanton who is hiding from the wreckage she has caused.

After a month of storm and fury, the sea lay frothing about the Hill of Fate, licking its grey base as a lion licks his wounds. It stretched out for leagues white with foam, coloured here and there with wreckage and masses of straying seaweed, with planks, weeds, and dead bodies of birds. Strewn amid the rocks to the north, along the shore at Rooruck, where the cliff fell away into a long uneven battlement of huge boulders, there was more wreckage. It was said that three mangled corpses were seen tangled among the rocks at Firbolg's Point. Sean Mor, who saw them, fled in fear, and when the villagers came they were washed away again by the tide. Farther north again, just south of the point where the waters of the north and south joined to travel eastwards, where the swift current seemed to suck the waves downwards to some cavern in the depths, three horses lay on a rock, lying on their sides, their stiff legs extended hairlessly, their bellies expanded, their nostrils full of sand.

The people feared the resting bilious sea as a soldier fears the silence of the guns in an interval between two engagements. When it raged, churned by the wind, it showed its might, but now the huge claws of its breakers were hidden in its frothing back. And they might shoot forth any moment. The sea might rise suddenly far away to the west and come towering in, each forked wave-crest a magnet that drew the sea before it into its hollow breast, until the Giants' Reef lay bared for a mile and the slimy insects clinging to its back stared gasping at the awe-inspiring sky, before the retreating sea again enveloped them in accustomed darkness. For the battle is not as fearsome as the waiting for it, nor is the sword as terrible as the fire in the eye that guides it. So the peasants feared the sea, and fearing it blessed it as their generous mother, who wrecked ships afar off to give them planks and barrels of oil and manila ropes and bales of cotton. They prowled about the shores and among the boulders beneath the Hill of Fate looking for wreckage.

By day the sun shone fitfully on Rooruck, coming laggardly over the high cliff of Coillnamhan Fort. Its shadows glistened through the mist and through the clouds that pursued it. By night the hoar-frost covered the earth, eating into the gashes that the wind had made. Wild starry nights were those nights in Inverara. Boys sat by their windows, shivering in

their shirts, afraid to sleep because of the strange noises
of falling seas that came from the Fountain Hole, where
the mermaids were said to weep for lost lovers as they
combed their long golden hair, dipping the combs in
the black brine that dripped from the roof of their cave
into the Purple Pool beneath. Wild starry nights, when
men dream of death and stillness, as they watch the
shivering moon fleeing through the scratched sky.
Death, death, death, and drear winds blowing around
frozen dead hearts, that once throbbed with love.
Inverara in winter is the island of death, the island of
defeated peoples, come thither through the ages over
the sea pursued by their enemies. Their children sit on
the cliffs dreaming of the past of their fathers,
dreaming of the sea, the wind, the moon, the stars, the
scattered remnants of an army, the remains of a feast
eaten by dogs, the shattering of a maniac's ambition.

The Stranger, lying on his bed in Red John's cabin,
was near to death. He had fallen into Little Mary's
arms when she opened the door, roused by the noise of
his fall against it.

'Ah, Mother of Christ,' she gasped once, seeing his
white face with the hair streaming over it, soddened by
the rain, as if he were dead. She thought he was dead.
She raised him in her strong arms like a child and ran
with him to his room, panting. Throwing him on the
bed she ran her hands wildly over his body, searching
for life in him. And then when she felt his heart beating
she raised her hands to heaven and thanked God and
wept with joy. She put him to bed and chafed his limbs
with turpentine. Then she rolled the blankets about
him and sat with her arm under his head, watching
until he should regain consciousness.

Dawn had just broken. Red John got up and came into the kitchen in his bare feet.

'Where is that – ' he began when he saw his wife through the open door of the Stranger's room, her arms around the Stranger's neck, her cheek to his lips. His small eyes narrowed and he clenched his hands. He moved stealthily to the door and looking in grinned viciously. 'Ha, now I have you, adulteress,' he hissed. But when she looked up at him he crept back terrified. There was no fear or shame or anger in her look. There was a sadness in her eyes, a distant look of sadness, as if she were no longer conscious of her relationship with him as a wife, as if his memory had died and been forgotten in her fear for her lover who was ill.

Red John shut the door and held on to the latch with his two hands to keep away from the look in her eyes. His superstitious mind thought she had gone mad or had been 'taken by the fairies,' just as Sarah Halloran had some years before. A sea-serpent had leered at her as she was washing bags in a pool beneath the Hill of Fate, and ever afterwards she sat there all day watching the spot where the serpent disappeared, until one day, tearing her hair, she threw herself headlong from the cliff. So they believed in Rooruck, for who could not believe in magic by that drear sea in winter, listening to its moaning at night?

Red John ran to the hearth as he heard his wife come to the door.

'Get the doctor, Red John,' she said.

Her voice was as gentle as the voice of a mother talking to her first-born. It was the first time he had heard her speak gently to him since they were married. Then she went back again to the Stranger without waiting for his reply. She felt a power within her that would make an army obey her command.

Red John stood by the hearth in his shirt, barefooted, scratching his thigh. He was struggling with two impulses, fear and jealousy: fear of the look he had seen in her eyes, and mad jealousy of her sitting with her arms around the Stranger's neck and her cheek to his lips.

'Let the bastard die,' he mumbled.

But again the memory of Sarah Halloran came to his mind and the ghost he himself had seen at the Monks' Well coming one night from Kilmurrage. He sat by the fire hugging his armpits, and became so much afraid of his wife being enchanted that he was unable to do anything. He didn't even hear her come rushing at him from the room until her hand was entwined in his hair and she hissed in his ear:

'Get the doctor quickly, or I will brain you.'

'Don't strike, woman,' he whined. 'I'm going.'

She watched while he dressed and left the cabin to get his pony. Soon he was riding down the rocky boreen through the village on to the road to Kilmurrage, waving the ends of the halter around his head and yelling to the mare like a madman. Little Mary stood at the door listening to the dying rattle of the horse's hoofs and she shuddered.

'Oh, cruel God, don't take him from me,' she cried, clasping her throat.

The sound of racing hoofs suggested to her her lover's death. That sound is the harbinger of death in Inverara in winter, heard at dawn or in the dead of night, when the sea is always devouring some one or shattering their limbs, and horses gallop in haste into

Kilmurrage with froth on their flanks, hurrying for the doctor and the priest. Women rush to their windows in their shifts and whisper, 'Lord between us and all harm, who is it has been drowned or who is hurt?'

Then she shut the door and went on tiptoe to the Stranger's bed, looking about her as if she were going to commit a shameful crime. She took a charm from her breast. Her mother had given it to her on her marriage day. It had been in her mother's family for countless generations. Her ancestry on the mother's side had all given their love freely and were superstitious, like all women who ask nothing of the world and are scorned for so doing. She laid the charm on the bed. She filled a cup with water and laid it on a chair beside the bed. Then she pressed the charm to her heart and kissed it. It was a square flat piece of yellowish stone covered with inscriptions, supposed to be written in Ogham Craombh, the old Druidic writing. Her mother had told her that the charm itself had originally been given to a Firbolg princess as the price of her love by a Tuatha De Danaan warrior, and that it had power to save its owner's lover from death or the designs of the devil. And who knows? One thing is as certain as another and nothing is reasonable. All men and women fashion their own gods, and they are all omnipotent.

Three times she dipped the stone in the water and three times she pressed it to the Stranger's lips, praying to Crom. And strangely enough, after the third pressure he stirred, then turned on his side and opened his eyes. She hastily hid the stone in the little embroidered packet that hung between her breasts, suspended by a silk string. As she buttoned her bodice she turned to him and smiled. He smiled too, fleetingly, as if he had been dreaming. Then the smile died quickly, like a gleam of sunshine followed by rain on a wet day in spring. He started. His limbs quivered, and he clutched at the clothes.

'What noise is that I hear?' he cried with a wild look in his eyes.

'It is nothing,' said Little Mary, 'but the high tide beating on the Jagged Rock. Perhaps it is the noises of your dreams you hear.'

'The noises of my dreams? What do you mean? What happened to me?'

She began to tell him. Her voice had a ringing sweet sound totally different to her usual voice when talking to Red John. The resonance of each word seemed to stand in the air for a moment after she had spoken the word. So it seemed to the Stranger. He listened to that after-sound without hearing the words she was uttering. His imagination, strained by the fit that was upon him, thought that she was a spirit.

'Ha,' he said to himself, 'I don't believe in spirits.'

Then suddenly he felt a queer sensation in his head, as if something were going to snap within the roof of his skull, just inside. He sat up in bed and strained out his hands to the full extent of his arms. He was afraid something was going to happen. He did not know what. Death? The thought came suddenly and he screamed with fright.

'What is it?' cried Little Mary, her face white with fear.

She rushed to his side, clutched him about the waist, and put her face up to his. He clutched her in turn, but his eyes wandered over her body without seeing her.

The vision of death was before his eyes. He could see his own corpse lying stiff and naked. He was waiting for that thing to snap within his skull. Where would he go then? What was there beyond? He had mocked death. He had told himself that he was eager to end the misery of existence. Death, death, yes death, but not like this. Like what then? With his boots on? In battle? But his memory, clear and scornful in that dread moment of waiting, taunted him with the fact that he had feared it just as much in battle. He had trembled with fear when the shells burst near him, and at night when he heard the dull sound of tunnelling under his feet. Christ! where was his philosophy?

'Little Mary,' he moaned, 'I don't want to die.'

As he uttered the words 'to die' his voice rose almost to a shriek, as if he were afraid even to hear himself talk of death.

'You will not die,' she said calmly. But she clung to him more closely, for she too was afraid. She was not afraid of death, but of life without her lover. Her strong healthy body could not imagine death.

'No, I will not die,' he said, but even as he said it, he felt more afraid. The fright spread all over his limbs as if he had conscious nerve-centres everywhere. The soles of his feet itched. His feet and shins felt as if needles were being thrust rapidly into them. He thought his heart was going to burst. Then his lungs were expanding. Then his throat swelled. Then his eyes commenced to move straight forward from his head. Then there was a complete stoppage of all his organs. His body went rigid. There was a tense moment of waiting, wondering when it would happen, his death. But just when he reached that point his reason began to work again. It began to work like a clock that stops mysteriously for a moment in the stillness of the night and begins to work again of its own accord. Thought flashed across his mind, cool and cunning. It mocked his fear. 'Bah,' he said with a laugh, 'what was I talking about? Get me a drink!'

While she was away for the drink, he lay on his back thinking. His reason kept tormenting him. 'There you are,' it said. 'You wanted to die, but now that death threatens you, you are afraid to die.' He tried to deny that. His vanity said that he did not fear death itself, but the uncertainty of what came after it, that he hated to die because he had not done any of the things he might have done. 'With my ability I could have done ... oh damn it.' Again he began to reason out what would happen to him if that thing did snap in his brain and he died. By the time Little Mary came back with the drink he had forgotten about himself altogether and was debating whether the Monistic conception of the Universe were the correct one. He had just decided that 'that idea,' he did not know very clearly what it was, was far more terrible than complete annihilation, when Little Mary put her hand under his head and held a drink to his lips.

'Drink this,' she said.

He gulped down the hot milk and then suddenly he felt grateful to her. He became clearly conscious of her presence beside him and it gave him a peculiar sense of cleanliness. It was the first awakening of his clean youth in him, of the Fergus O'Connor who lived a clean life before his father's death turned him towards cynicism and debauchery. He had always been that way, a prey to impulses. He could contemplate with equanimity the destruction of a race, and yet he would remember the generosity of a tramp and to hurt a fly caused him physical pain.

He looked up at her and touched her hand. He tried to say something, but he couldn't. His throat went dry and he flushed. He saw her beauty as a pure thing, too, for the first time. It made him feel ashamed of himself, her beauty. He let go her hand hurriedly.

While he held her hand Little Mary blushed deeply. Until then she had been as cool and collected as a hospital nurse. But the pressure of his hand sent a warm thrill through her body. She wanted to lie down and close her eyes. The fierceness of passion that filled her while he was unconscious of her presence left her. As soon as he noticed her with even a glance of the eye and a pressure of the hand her womanly instincts forced her to shrink from him, blushing. She retired to the chair at the head of the bed and sat down; her hands trembled as she fastened the neck of her bodice she had left undone when she hurriedly put back the charm. Her face shivered spasmodically as if she were swallowing something indescribably sweet.

They waited in silence until the doctor came. Shy even to think of him now, she listened in rapt attention to the noise of the water dripping into the barrel placed at the gable, to catch the water that dripped from the roof. He lay thinking of many things. His weary brain stared at this new sensation, so different to any he had felt before, this sensation of being purified by the presence of a beautiful woman, of being cared for, of being protected spiritually. Like wild nature outside, lying bare in its winter sleep, his soul rested. So they waited, resting, he, she and nature, as if they were waiting in silence together for the beginning of life.

The noise of horse's hoofs came to them from the lane. The sounds were uneven as of a horse ridden by an unskilled rider. Then loud shouting was heard and Little Mary ran out. The pony was standing at the door. He was champing at the bit and kicking his belly with his right hind leg, for never in his life before had a saddle touched his back or a bit been in his mouth. In Inverara it was considered unmanly to use anything on a horse but a rope halter, and a rough blanket to protect the crutch from the horse's spine. The new doctor sat on the pony's back, Dr. Cassidy's successor (Dr. Cassidy had been forced to retire in his eightieth year because of a petition being lodged with the County Council by the islanders). The new doctor was from Dublin. He considered himself an important person and therefore always insisted on riding a saddled horse to visit a patient. Being too mean to buy a horse and feed it, he bought a cheap saddle and reins instead and compelled the islanders to bring him their horses for his use. He sat on the pony's back, a white muffler wound many times around his neck, in brand-new russet riding-breeches and gaiters like an English sportsman in a film picture. He wore a hard bowler hat perched on his square head. The trimmest of clipped moustaches covered his upper lip. He cracked his whip timorously, taking care not to touch the mare with it. He sat there waiting, either because he was unable to dismount without assistance or because he considered it proper for a gentleman to wait until somebody held the stirrup. They called him Dr. Aloysius Rogan at the post office and on Government papers, but the peasants called him 'the Son of the Potman,' because they said his father kept a public-house in the Dublin slums.

Little Mary helped him to dismount. He leaned against her more heavily than was necessary. In his own estimation he was 'a devil among the girls,' and he had 'his eye on Little Mary' for a long time. A group of peasants that had rushed out of their cabins as soon as the arrival of the doctor was reported by a dirty boy who had been digging for a rat in the fence beside the road, gathered around Red John's Gate, spitting from their throats needlessly and rubbing the backs of their hands across their mouths. The doctor paused a moment to inquire the name of the village, although he knew it quite well, and then entered the cabin. The peasants leaned over the fence and passed disparaging remarks on the doctor, the saddle, and on Red John for not tightening his mare's hind shoes.

'Does he think a horse is a donkey, the son of a lame monk?' said one.

'Who the devil is sick, God forgive us?' said another.

'It's the Stranger, and no wonder God would stiffen his blasphemous tongue,' said another.

'No, no, curly Stephen,' said another, 'sure it's the war has stricken the poor man. He bought me a drink the other night. He is good-natured and God-fearing.'

'Begob,' said a large-eared man with a coarse laugh, 'I thought it was how Red John had brought his boat into port at last,' meaning that he thought Red John was about to become the father of a family. They all laughed.

The doctor stood for fully a minute in the kitchen taking off his gloves. He smelt the walls all round like an excise officer smelling for illicit whisky. He handed his gloves to Little Mary and looked at her deeply as she took them. Then the Stranger's voice came from the room harshly.

'Who the devil is that, Little Mary?' he cried.

The doctor arched his eyebrows and shrugged his shoulders. He went to the door of the Stranger's room and thrust in his head and right foot like a man going to visit a prize sow in a pigsty. He saw the Stranger lying on the bed, the long pale hands lying over the coverlet, the black eyes gleaming, looking fiercely at him, the brown beard giving the face the expression of a beachcomber. He shrugged his shoulders again and advanced into the room. His face was set in an expression that he had studied in the Dublin hospitals when he realized that his abilities would never allow him to aim any higher than a practice among peasants or in the slums. It was a disdainful, condescending expression.

'Well, my man,' he said, 'how do you feel?' Then without waiting for an answer he turned to Little Mary and said, 'Does the sea ever come down as far as this from the beach? What did you say the village was called? Ro-ro-rooy, oh! Funny name.' Then immediately he forgot Little Mary and his question, began to whistle 'Over the waves,' took from his shoulders the shooting-bag that held his instruments and began to open it on the table. Little Mary stared at him with a brooding expression in her eyes, as if he were a dangerous animal. The Stranger turned on his side and glared at him. He was fuming inwardly against 'this impertinent fellow,' but he was afraid to say anything. He was more afraid of death than he was insulted by the attitude of the doctor. Would the doctor be able to assist him? Would he be able to cure that catching in the chest, when the heart beat too quickly? Would he be able to stop the trembling of the limbs when fear struck him? Would he be able to dispel the visions from the brain? He was ashamed too of the position in which the doctor found him, lying in the cabin of a peasant. He struggled between shame and fear and hope and anger on the bed, until at last the doctor approached him with a stethoscope. Then he felt a desire to jump up and strangle the doctor, in order to rid himself of this complex tangle of emotions by some sudden physical act. But that impulse vanished immediately. He felt a kind of careless resignation, much the same as the soldier feels when he is being court-martialled and he knows that no effort of will or of body or no strength of evidence will have any effect on the stupidity of his judges or on the mighty machine that they control.

The doctor sounded his chest and back. He tapped his knees. He put his hand before his eyes, ordering him to look at a point on the wall in a voice one would use talking to a stone man. He looked at his tongue and put a lens down his jaws and peered at it. He tapped the teeth casually with the lens. He pressed his finger against the cheekbones and watched the blood crawling back over the whitened space. He felt the pulse and whistled like an engine thudding and tapped his foot in time with the tune as he took the count. He felt his loins and asked him did he ever have venereal disease. Then he threw the clothes back over the body with a sigh, went to the table and laid down his instruments. The Stranger lay trembling, resignedly accepting all this contumely in his fear of death. He stopped breathing, waiting for the doctor's verdict.

'Nothing the matter with you that I can see,' said the doctor, lighting a cigarette. 'Been drinking too much and you are suffering from acute indigestion. Just come back from the United States? A relative of these people?' He waved the match in Little Mary's direction.

The Stranger, having discovered that there was no danger of immediate death and that his fears were all fantasies, now boiled with rage against 'this lout of a fellow.' He grew choleric. His lips twitched and his nostrils curved upwards like a dog going to snarl. But he could say nothing. Still the doctor was absolutely unmoved.

'Sorry, my man,' he said. 'One gets irritable in a place like this. That sea must be lonely at nights. Dreadful place. Wonder the Government doesn't ... Ah yes, this will be ... yes, h'm ... Let's say ten shillings. I'll send you a bottle. A spoonful three times a day. The – er – your husband, I believe, my good woman, will – er – take it over to you. And by crikey, I'd advise you to stop drinking.'

'Get me my purse,' said the Stranger to Little Mary. 'You'll find it in the portmanteau there. There, there, that black one. Quick.' He snapped his fingers, eager to pay the doctor and get him out of the room before he should lose control of himself and strangle him. 'The ass,' he muttered to himself, sitting up in bed, twitching his toes and gripping the blanket with his hands, waiting for his purse. 'To think that I must be insulted by a fellow like that. Great Scott, is this the way they treat everybody? Great Christ, if I could only

beat his face into a pulp.' He took a ten-shilling note
from his purse with trembling hands and threw it to
the doctor without speaking. The doctor caught it
deftly between his fingers as it fluttered to the floor. He
carelessly packed his bag, slung it on his shoulder, said
'Good morning, you'll be all right in a few days,' and
left the room, followed by Little Mary.

The Stranger lay on the bed without moving, with
the notecase in his hands. He suddenly took out the
notes and counted them. As he was not going to die, he
had an interest in his material wealth, and he put his
hand to his chin.

'Wait now,' he mused; 'I have paid for a year's board
and lodging to Red John. Good job I did that. I'm safe
for a year. And let me see: twenty, twenty-five, thirty,
forty, forty-five, fifty, fifty-three pounds ... ten and
there are a few shillings in my trousers pockets.' He
put the notes back and gripped the purse between his
fingers. He must look after that money. Life was sweet
after all. It would be all right living in Rooruck ... away
from the world. Just living without any effort. God
knows what he might not discover about life sitting up
there on the Hill of Fate. 'Say, supposing I was sent
here by fate to discover something wonderful!' He
became enthusiastic.

Then Little Mary came in and he handed her the
purse. She was smiling, glad that he was not seriously
ill. The white streaks in her grey eyes were shining
brightly as she smiled.

'Thank God, you'll be all right,' she said. 'He told me
to get you a drop of brandy for the pain in your
stomach. He said it was wind. I'll run down to
Derrane's and see have they got any.'

'Don't be long away, Mary,' he called after her as she went. He was afraid of being alone. As soon as she had left the house he became worried again. His enthusiasm vanished. He suspected that the doctor had told him a lie. What did the doctor care? He recalled stories he had heard of doctors letting people die without making the least effort to save them. He felt that he was deserted by the world, that nobody cared whether he lived or died, that he was unable to help himself, that there was nobody bound to him by ties of blood. He heard the sea rumble. He felt a morose satisfaction in the thought that it was licking its jaws, preparing to devour him. Then the thought came to him that he would die at night, alone in his room. The wind would sing a cunning hissing song, trying to calm his fears so that the sea would crawl up unawares and devour him. Then all those black cormorants that he had seen on the jagged Reef would strain out their twisted long necks and tear pieces from his carcass. They would swallow the pieces without chewing them and tear again. Then he discovered himself counting the number of cormorants that were tearing at his body and he tried to shout. But he was too agitated to shout. He crept down under the blankets and commenced to cry. He felt sorry that he couldn't pray to God without losing his self-respect. It would be such a comfort to throw himself on the mercy of some Being that was stronger than nature. There was no use appealing to nature. Nature was too strong and just to be influenced by prayer. Then he remembered Little Mary. 'Great God,' he murmured, 'that woman is good to me.' Then to hide from himself the fact that he wanted her near him because he was ill and helpless, he told himself that he was very fond of her and he became jealous of her husband.

When she brought him the brandy he thanked her with tears in his eyes. She wanted to put her arms about him and embrace him, but instead she drew away to the window and pulled the curtain over it.

'Go to sleep now,' she whispered. She tiptoed to the door. She was closing the door when he asked her to leave it open. He wanted to hear her moving in the kitchen. He was afraid of being alone. He watched her move around the kitchen for a time and then he became sleepy as the brandy warmed his stomach. He lay prone and closed his eyes. He heard Red John coming into the kitchen, shuffling and grumbling.

'Hey then, woman, there's a journey for you, and the son of a loose woman never gave me a drink. Hey then, there's a doctor for you.'

'Be quiet there, you pest,' said Little Mary.

'Hey then, whose house is this, cracked woman?'

Then he heard Red John talking in a loud voice outside the door to somebody about the weather. 'I would say in spite of the four Gospels if they were laid on my palm that the wind has veered southward a point,' Red John was saying.

The Stranger wondered for a few moments where Red John had heard of the four Gospels, or if he knew what they were about, and if he did read them, would he think them credible? He decided that Red John would spit and say 'Huh' when he had finished reading the Gospels. Then he fell asleep.

He awoke at intervals during the day. The kitchen was full of peasants, men and women, every time he awoke. The peasants of Rooruck, like all peasants and rustics and small townspeople, loved the sensation of somebody in their village being dead or sick or murdered or accused of murder or gone mad. They did not read newspapers, so the pleasure of talking scandal and trying to foist crimes and immoral habits on each other was their only harmless pleasure. But they were willing to pay for their pleasure. They brought Little Mary jugs of milk, round 'hillocks' of butter, and dried fish as gifts for the 'sick man.' The men sat near the door on a wooden bench, with their elbows on their knees, spitting everywhere. The women huddled themselves like Turks on the floor, with their hands clasped in front of their shins. They would sit in silence for a long time, pitching from side to side uneasily, like sheep being eaten by maggots. They rolled their eyes around vigorously to examine everything. Then they went away and gathered in groups around the village. They talked for hours with their heads close together, hugging their elbows like wicked Chinamen in a film tragedy.

'Lord save us, the way Little Mary looks at one.'

'Did you notice anything, O wife of Lame Peter?'

'I did, but I wouldn't like to mention it.'

'Ye needn't be afraid. I noticed the same thing myself.'

'You mean to say that –'

'Yes, that's the very thing I said to myself as soon as I entered the house.'

'It should be stopped.'

'A fine-built woman like that not to have a child. It's the curse of God that struck her barren.'

It was about midnight when the Stranger awoke. He felt refreshed. When his consciousness fully awakened and he remembered the events of the day before, he felt a strange happiness. It appeared to him that he had escaped a great catastrophe. He sat up in bed with his hands about his knees, contemplating himself.

Nature was still, except for the distant quarrelling of the sea, as if the waves were complaining at being forced to keep vigil over sleeping nature. It was so still that he thought the world was dead. 'This is the turning-point in my life,' he said, nodding his head and frowning as if he were stating an irrefutable fact. Then he began to think with remarkable clarity. He fancied that he could see his brain thinking. It appeared to him to be like a crystal with amorphous ideas glinting within it. He wanted to poke his fingers into its sides like a boy watching goldfish in a glass. Then he lay back from the contemplation of his brain and became aware of the power and vastness of nature. 'I am a part of nature.' Before, he had considered himself superior to nature. Now it struck him that he was merely a component part of the universe, just an atom, with less power than the smallest fleck of foam that was snatched by the wind from the nostrils of an advancing wave. Ha! Then he belonged to something. There was a mother too between whose breasts he could hide his head, a mother more powerful than a thousand gods. Just fancy. He could surrender himself to nature without fear. He smiled, confident that he had solved the puzzle of life. Now death could hold no terror for him, since after death he would return to nature and nature was immortal. It always moved, and motion was life. He listened to the voice of the sea eagerly, as to the voice of a father. He pictured it tumbling in among the rocks, beds of seaweed swimming in the white surf. He heard its crash as it struck the base of the cliffs. He saw the fountain of surf rising, hissing as it rose to a slender curving point. He saw it fall backwards into the retreating wave that scurried in and out among the long-toothed rocks as if it had been blinded and had lost its way. He saw it drivelling into pools and then rush with a subdued roar into the body of the ocean, to join another wave that towered higher and higher as it advanced, green and menacing. Ha! It moved without purpose. That was life, motion without purpose.

He jumped up in bed and cried in an awed whisper, 'By God, I've found it!' He judged the world in the light of his discovery, that life was motion without purpose. His brain had a weird faculty for presenting things to him vividly, as clearly as if they were filmed. He watched the tens of millions of people in cities striving for wealth, power and fame, sacrificing everything to gain honour and property. He laughed outright, heartily. It was the most ridiculous farce he had ever looked at. He held his sides laughing. He began to imitate them. He saw a fat-bellied man rising at a Business Dinner. 'Gentlemen!' he said, 'I can confidently assert that James Buchanan is a man who will leave his mark on the pages of the world's history. His self-sacrifice, his indomitable courage, his business acumen, his untiring energy, his . . .' 'Oh hell,' gurgled the Stranger, 'now I understand Rabelais!' He saw others, lean-faced men, with anger in their eyes and hunger in their stomachs, shouting at the fat-bellied men, agitating for revolution and liberty, shouting about ideals and principles, honour, self-sacrifice, brotherly love! They were still more ridiculous. Did the sea have principles? Did the wind rise and tear down houses inspired by ideas? Did the rain flood towns, inspired by the spirit of self-sacrifice? Did the waves consider themselves in honour bound to wreck ships? 'Pish! It's motion without purpose,' he said, turning on his side to have a better view of the idiots. He nestled his hands between his thighs. And now the world presented the appearance of a lunatic asylum. Demented people were running about, grinning like apes, shouting at one another, puffing out their chests, turning somersaults like small boys from school on a holiday. One man came running with a manuscript in his hand. 'I am a genius,' he cried. 'See this book I have written!' The manuscript rolled page after page before the Stranger's eyes. He read every word in a trice. He saw vermin crawling on the beautiful heroine's corpse even before she had fallen into her lover's arms in the last paragraph. Then another man appeared, with something in a little glass tube. 'Hey! you people,' he cried, 'hey you, look at me. I'm the devil of a scientist! I have discovered a cure for all diseases. Man will soon be immortal.' And he had scarcely finished speaking when he got run over by a motor-car and got killed. A fat general with bandy legs, a fierce moustache and a sloping forehead came along. He stood squat and roared like a bull until his lungs almost burst and his face was red and choleric. 'This is General Dictator speaking,' he shouted. 'I have killed a million of the enemy. Now let liberty reign and peace.' The millions flung their hats in the air, when a huge wave rose playfully and enveloped all the millions! Then the whole world froze up and skidded off through space. Another planet had collided with it.

The Stranger was laughing at his vision when he suddenly became vexed with the folly of the world. 'What a scoundrelly farce!' he muttered. 'And look at all the good men it deceives!' There was no end, no goal, no certainty, except in living aimlessly. Nothing was assured but the air, the earth and the sea. He fancied that he could see the cormorants sitting stupidly on the jagged Rock, bobbing their heads lazily. 'We have lived here five hundreds of years,' they croaked sardonically. 'And we have heard it all, all before now! but tell us what does it end in? In ashes and oblivion?'

Then having torn the veil of sanity from the face of the mad world he turned on himself. He had been just as insane as the others whom he despised, trying to create a purpose in life. He had considered himself a genius and was enraged with his fellows for ignoring him. 'Fancy being vexed with people whom you despise!' Ha, he could laugh at them all now!

Then, having satisfied his vanity, he stopped thinking. He listened for sounds in the house. He felt a slight thirst and thought he would call out for some brandy. But he immediately found that he did not feel thirsty but hungry. He was so glad at feeling hungry that he flopped down flat in the bed, snored and fell asleep immediately.

Little Mary, sitting by the kitchen fire, keeping vigil over him, heard the creaking of the bed and tiptoed to the room door.

'Do you want anything?' she whispered.

Hearing no reply she moved softly to the bed and heard him sleeping calmly. She brushed her hand

lightly over his hair and went back to the fire again.
She sat half-sleeping, half-dreaming of love, arranging
the minutest detail of her future life with her lover. Her
dreams all began with the day they would fly from
Inverara together. Before that day there was a vast
wilderness in which she could see nothing.

When the Stranger awoke next morning he felt
better. There was nothing but a slight twitching at the
knees when, in spite of himself, his mind scurried into
the past for a fleeting moment. He ate ravenously.
Little Mary stood beside him while he ate, hoping that
he would give her a glance of recognition. But he had
forgotten all about her as soon as his fit had vanished.
She was again to him but a peasant woman who was
handing him his food. Her eyelashes drooped. Her lips
quivered. She was debating in her mind whether she
hated or loved him. She wanted to hate him, but she
couldn't. But she made an irritated gesture as she
swept away the remains of his breakfast. He did not
notice it. He noticed nothing but himself. He lay back
and smoked a pipe.

'I am a new man,' he thought. 'I'm finished with the
past. I think I will get up and walk around the shore. I
will look at the sea.' He put on his clothes and walked
into the kitchen. But then he got dizzy and Little Mary
had to help him to a seat.

Little Mary was arranging a couch for him by the
fire when Red John came in.

'How does the sea look to-day?' asked the Stranger.

Red John growled, 'It looks very well,' and spat into
the fire. He sat in the opposite corner with his head
between his hands. Since he had seen his wife by the
Stranger's bedside with the bewitched look in her eyes,

his mind was troubled with queer and terrible
thoughts. He wanted to kill his wife, but he was afraid
to do so. The good God forbade it. And in what other
way could he get rid of her? What were the neighbours
saying about him? Great Virgin of the Valiant Deeds!
how they'd laugh at him if they found his wife was in
love with the Stranger! As he sat by the fire he thought
of the fat widow in Kilmillick who had fifteen acres of
land, whom he knew was willing to marry him. Had
she not whispered to him one night in Kilmurrage that
it was lonely sleeping alone in winter. And Kilmillick
was a better village in every way than Rooruck. He had
heard Sean Mor prove it one night in Mulligan's
publichouse. But how was he to get rid of his wife? Eh?
He looked at the Stranger furtively over his beard and
then jumped to his feet and muttered as he went out of
the door, 'To the devil with it for a story.'

'What is that he said, Little Mary?' said the Stranger.

'Oh, don't mind him,' she said, fussing anxiously
about the room. She swore to herself that she would
thrash her husband at the first opportunity.

But the Stranger felt uneasy. He realized that Red
John was jealous of him. He thought that he was
making a fool of himself with Little Mary. 'But good
God! I have done nothing,' he told himself. It was
ridiculous to think that he would have 'an affair' with
her. 'She is good to me and that is all,' he thought. But
even as he thought that his passion became slightly
aroused. But it died again immediately. His body was
very weak. He laughed lowly and thought, 'What a
fool I am!' Little Mary looked at him and he said to her
with a laugh, 'Oh well, of course I know he didn't
mean anything.' But they both blushed as they looked

at one another, as if they were conscious of having
something to hide from Red John.

He passed the day quietly thinking by the fire, flying
from one field of thought to another sleepily. At one
moment he felt happy and certain of everything; at
another moment he felt gloomy and in doubt. He
reacted to every sound that he heard from outside. At
one moment it was a boy riding a donkey down the
lane; the wild yells of the boy rose triumphantly after
each hissing lash of a dried sea rod across the donkey's
flank. And the donkey's hoofs tipped the ground
slowly in jingling succession as if he were not being hit.
A flock of seagulls whirled screaming over the village.
A peasant woman called out 'Ho-e-e-e-e White
Anthony, what news have you got?' Then all sounds
would die, except the sounds of the sea, thr-r-up, flup,
hsssss. Then a cock would crow sadly. And he wove
trains of thought about all these sounds. Night brought
him sound sleep. His mind was shrouded by a kind of
birth bag that shut out the world. The past was
becoming unreal and distant. The sea was singing a
crooning song in his ears that lulled him to sleep. It
was a sad song, like the songs that mothers sing to their
babes in Inverara, where all joy is the depth of sadness
in winter. It was the joyous sadness of those who grow
to despise joy in their sorrow. There was a half-smile
on his lips as he was falling asleep. The wind coming
down the slope of Coillnamhan Fort from the east was
the last sound he heard. It played somnolent music on
the grey smooth crags, epics of races dead a million
years, a moment in its ageless life. It sang them with a
jeer at the end of each blast, jeering at effort and

ambition. He stretched out his legs, crossed his feet and slept.

Next morning he sat once more by the fire. He had no energy. He wanted to sit quietly and listen to life moving about him. He shuddered when he saw Red John come in after a night hunting for wreckage, drenched to the skin by the ice-cold sea-water. He had been fighting the other peasants for two barrels of paraffin oil that had been washed ashore and he had got nothing. Red John walked up and down by the door stamping his wet feet and saying 'huh' now and again viciously. He began to curse the other peasants, gesticulating.

'That son of a wanton, Patch the son of Bartly, prevented me from getting the second barrel,' he cried, spitting out of the door. He crouched around the floor describing the struggle for the barrel. He had gone out to his waist to meet a huge wave. He had his hand on the barrel as it was carried past him. Then the wave swept the barrel and himself fifty feet along the weed-covered rocks. He was knocked into a pool. The barrel was sweeping back again towards him on the backwash of the wave, when Patch the son of Bartly, his eyes starting from his head with greed, rushed in front of him. Clinging with one hand to a ledge of rock Red John was about to grasp the barrel with the other hand when Patch threw himself upon it with a yell, shouting, 'Let go, let go, it's mine!' And then they both struggled and the barrel was carried out along the rocks until Michael the son of Littie Michael grappled it with a hook. 'I'll have his life yet, the son of a wanton,' cried Red John furiously. Then without changing his clothes he took a pitchfork and went out to gather seaweed on the pebbly beach that stretched along the north of Rooruck towards Coillnamhan.

Little Mary was at the well beetling clothes, and the Stranger sat by the fire shivering, glad that he did not have to go out to fight for barrels. It made him afraid of life, that fierce struggle on the wild beach.

'I wish Little Mary would come,' he muttered. He felt lonely. He listened to the splashing sound of her beetle falling on the clothes and counted the strokes, wondering when she would have finished and come back to him. 'Why do I want her?' he cried angrily. 'I'm all right, eh? I don't want anybody.' He began to excuse himself for wanting her near him. Yes, it was nothing more than her company. Nothing more. It would be utterly disgraceful falling in love with her. 'Love?' he cried aloud. Then he laughed harshly. 'Go on, O'Connor! You are a fool. An utter idiot. I just want to talk to the woman. I must talk to somebody.' He waited until she came back. 'Sit down, Little Mary,' he said, 'I want to talk to you.' Little Mary took her knitting and sat near him quietly. Her face bore the expression of a man preparing for confession.

He began to talk, listening to his own voice excitedly. He debated abstruse problems. He asked himself questions as he talked. He threw out theories as his own and began to refute them as if they were set up by an enemy. Now and again he asked Little Mary, 'Do you understand that?' She nodded her head in silence and looked at him with a smile from under her lashes. But she never understood a word of what he was saying. She was watching the play of his lips as he spoke, feeling that she wanted to kiss them. She was debating with herself what would put 'some flesh on his body.' She was wondering how he would make love to her if she could only arouse his passion. She smiled instinctively in the right place or nodded her head or shrugged her shoulders, in order that he might think she was listening to him and be pleased with her. Then the Stranger disarranged the pillows under his back in the heat of an argument with himself and she jumped up to settle them comfortably. The Stranger paused suddenly with open mouth. He had reached what he thought was a marvellous climax to a chain of reasoning. He was denouncing the cupidity of an American millionaire who had rushed from success to success, until at last the dreary accumulation of his satisfied mercenary desires drove him to . . . And just then when he expected Little Mary to be waiting eagerly for the climax she jumped up to arrange his pillows. 'Bah!' he thought, 'she is a stupid peasant. She doesn't understand me. I must go and have a talk to O'Daly. I can talk to him. He is a man of the world.' But he sat moodily by the fire for another hour, unable to rouse his energy.

Then the wind began to sigh more loudly. Cows lowed. The sea crashed heavily against the southern cliffs. The dim shadows of day crept up closer to the door of the cabin. Night was falling. He jumped to his feet. 'Get me an oilskin coat, Mary,' he said, 'I want to go to Coillnamhan.'

She started, afraid that he was going to Carmody's public-house.

'Oh, don't go drinking again,' she said beseechingly, standing near him.

'Go on, get me the coat,' he said angrily.

She forgot her shyness of him and caught him by the breast. She pressed close to him and looked fondly into his eyes. He felt her hot sweet breath on his face. Unconsciously he put his arms about her and kissed her red lips. But even as his lips touched hers, his mind was far away contemplating a million men kissing a million women aimlessly. The soft suction of her lips burying themselves in his repelled him. He put her from him and stroked her hair. She stood motionless. Then he snatched his coat from its peg and went out. And as he strode away down the lane he felt proud of his conquest of her, and he smiled. But coming out on the highroad he halted and bit his lip. His conscience pricked him for having kissed her. He cracked his fingers and frowned. 'She's an excellent woman to me, I must look after her,' he said, and walked on, as if he were an omnipotent God who could perform a miracle or blast a kingdom with the snapping of a finger.

But still the kiss pursued him. He kept wiping his lips with his handkerchief as if it were a physical injury. He had kissed a hundred women, in cabarets, in cafés, even in brothels. He had made love sometimes with passion, sometimes boredly, always carelessly, forgetting the women nonchalantly after he had left them. Yet he now felt conscience-stricken after kissing this peasant woman. 'It's this damn island,' he growled. 'It's enchanted. Ugh!' Nature seemed to be leering at him viciously. He thought spirits were watching him among the black crags that loomed sombrely out of the darkness on either side of the white road, warning him against violating the mating law of nature. The sea was running sibilantly in and out on the sandy beach at Coillnamhan. It was cutting narrow deep gashes in the sand. He felt it was showing him how sharp its claws were. The wind came in little fawning rushes about his ears, like a cat tapping a mouse with furred claws before it suddenly drives its sharp teeth through the neck and growls as it hears the bones crunch. He said 'Phew' and walked faster. Then he cried aloud querulously, 'But, Great Scott, it was she herself ... but oh to hell with it, I'm going crazy. Ha, ha, ha!' Then he forgot about her and began to array in his mind the pet subjects that he wanted to discuss with O'Daly.

He heard sounds of music coming from O'Daly's cottage as he approached. He stood in wonder listening, drinking in the delicious sound that always intoxicated him. He realized this was classic music and he wondered who was playing. 'It's a violin,' he said. He became jealous of O'Daly for being able to play so well, for he himself could not play and he hated anybody being able to do anything which he himself could not do. He swore and knocked at the door. He waited for two minutes, but no answer came. The music still continued. Then a woman's voice began to accompany it. 'Ha, that's his daughter,' he said, and his heart began to throb. Her voice was sad and sweet. It seemed to mingle with the sounds of the wind and the sea. It would go forward for a space softly, sibilantly. Then it gathered strength and rose in a thickening wild cascade of sound, like a wave ridden by the wind breaking against a cliff. Then another clear note joined it at the height, a note of fierce unconquerable pride, that wound whirling steel bands about it. And immediately it fell, lower and lower, laughing, tingling, as if it were shivering in an ecstasy of ferocious joy, like the voice of a mad woman laughing over the dead body of her lover. A frenzy of passion rose within him as he listened. He longed to grasp a sword, to smite mountains, to heave huge weights, in order to exhaust the energy born in him by the music. He ran down the path away from the house. But as soon as he was out of reach of the music he stopped, snorting. He leaned over the gate, his perspiring body chilled. He looked back at the house as if it concealed enemies. He trembled with fear, thinking it was enchanted. The moon and myriads of stars made the night bright. The thatched cottage stood out clearly against the face of the low hill behind it, where the crag ended in a glen. The glen was covered with a shadowy mist, the gaunt bare trees standing about in it. He could hear the dull rumble of the spring water dripping from the base of the ivy-covered rock to the left. The roof of the cottage hung low, as if it staggered under its thatch. The rain had stained the yellow paint on the walls. Withered rose bushes lined each side of the little portico. 'Hell, I'm silly!' he said. 'I've seen hundreds of cottages like that. I'll go in.'

He walked steadily up to the door again and knocked. The music stopped. He heard a chair upset and then the door opened. O'Daly's daughter faced him in the hall. A lamp swinging over her enveloped her head in a bright light. Stray tresses of auburn hair rose quivering in the wind from the huge coil that lay banked about her forehead. They glistened as if sparks of fire had fallen from the lamp on them. Her eyes were just like her father's, blue, gleaming, fierce, cold eyes. Her face was like her father's. The lips were thin and compressed. The nose was straight and the nostrils were slightly distended. The rest of her body was slight. In her right hand she held the violin she had been playing.

'You are heartily welcome,' she said, bowing slightly. Her voice was cold, almost sharp, totally unlike the voice he had heard singing a minute before.

He said 'Thank you' and followed her into the sitting-room on the right.

The sitting-room was low-roofed and large. A turf fire burned brightly in a large black grate. A French window, with sloping bays, almost covered one side. A reading-lamp rested on a round mahogany table in the centre. The remaining walls were lined with books. The picture of a fierce-looking man, wearing sidewhiskers, hung over the fireplace. Evidently an O'Daly, and an ancient one, for he wore ruffles. O'Daly's head appeared over the back of a leather-covered armchair that was drawn up in front of the fire. The toes of his right foot, covered with a grey sock, also appeared over the back of the chair. It was resting on the low mantelpiece. O'Daly did not rise, but he wheezed and groaned, as he apologized for not rising. 'Rheumatism ... Meet my daughter Kathleen ... nearing my last ... heard you had the doctor ... sorry to hear it ... an awful scoundrel ... take your chair to the fire ... get that bottle of brandy, Kathleen.'

The Stranger sat opposite O'Daly. He cast a hesitating look after Kathleen as she walked slowly to the door, strumming her fingers along the table as she passed. He noticed she was wearing a knitted saffron dress, with a deep black band around the waist. Her slim body was as lithe as the body of a wild animal. The length of the fingers that strummed along the table made him stare after her, as she disappeared through the door. There was a deep hollow in the back of her neck beneath her piled-up hair and the hair grew thickly each side of the hollow. As he looked towards O'Daly from her he blushed. She was the first educated woman with whom he had come in contact for a long time. In fact he had never known the companionship of educated women. The kind who gave their love easily attracted him more. 'They were less waste of time,' he used to say. Now he felt embarrassed and attracted. He also felt ashamed of himself. He was looking at O'Daly for several seconds before he could see the man. O'Daly was making peculiar grimaces, jerking his face upwards slightly with his upper lip curled. Then he leaned over and whispered, grasping the Stranger's right knee, 'Be careful what you say. She is very religious. Gives me dog's abuse for swearing. I declare to Christ the women nowadays ... whist! here she comes.'

Kathleen entered the room with a tray, carrying a bottle and two glasses. As she filled the glasses in silence, she made grimaces as if the smell of the brandy were stifling her. She handed a glass to each of them and then sat by the table holding her handkerchief to her mouth.

O'Daly, with his glass half-raised to his lips, looked at her half-mournfully, half-fiercely, like an old dog after being beaten by a young master, and then he said, 'Phew. Here's a good health, Mr. O'Connor.' He drank. 'My daughter is a temperance woman,' he added. Kathleen shrugged her shoulders with a sigh, and they both looked at her. But nobody spoke. O'Daly swallowed the contents of his glass, but the Stranger put down his glass almost full. He knew Kathleen was watching him and he became oppressedly conscious of the dilapidated state of his clothes, his worn features, and ... though he hated to admit it ... of his sinful past. Then he began to talk to her; casually at first, while O'Daly glared furiously at each of them, cracked his fingers, made a noise like a man urging a horse, and swore under his breath, trying to find a more comfortable place in his chair. He was like a fish out of water in the presence of his religious, cultured and highly civilized daughter. But the Stranger, as soon as she began to talk to him, felt a stiffening that drove out his embarrassment. There was an aggressive yet pitying tone in her voice that maddened him. 'You've been to the University,' she said, rubbing the fingers of her right hand slowly along the back of the left.

He felt she was patronizing him.

'Yes,' he said curtly, 'I spent a few years in that den of superstition before I had sense enough to begin my education properly.'

O'Daly laughed loudly and then swore as he stubbed his toes trying to sit upright.

'Damn right,' he yelled, waving his beard in an ecstasy of self-enjoyment, 'the only place to learn is . . .' And then he stopped dead, meeting the cold stare of his daughter. He dropped down into his chair until only his arms protruded.

Kathleen looked at the Stranger with a half pitiful, half-contemptuous look. She looked from under her eyelashes and seemed to shiver inwardly in horror of such a statement.

'Oh,' she said, 'I see.'

The Stranger fumed. He understood quite well that she said several things after the manner women have of saying a thousand bitter things in a silent glance. She said, 'You have been in the British army and therefore you are an enemy of your country,' since she, like all cultured young Irish women, was a Nationalist for the same reason that similar types in other countries are suffragettes or followers of nature-cults or social reformers, to express their newly discovered sex freedom. She said, 'You are a pariah since you have lost your religion,' for as a cultured young Irish woman, the Christian religion was to her an emblem of purity, sex freedom, and a bulwark against everything gross and foreign. And the Stranger, even though his reason despised both Nationalism and Christianity as relics of the childhood of human thought, felt himself in the position of a man accused by his own family of heinous crimes against the family honour.

He began furiously to denounce everything – religion, Nationalism, civilization.

'Civilization,' he said, 'is only a plaster to hide sores. Priests are hirelings of the patriotic vampires who suck the blood of the people.'

He became eloquent, as Kathleen tried to refute his arguments. In Irish fashion they gesticulated, they struck the table, they said things they didn't mean to say, and they finally ended by forgetting what they began to discuss and lapsed into a heated silence.

O'Daly, who had stared open-mouthed at them during the argument, then jumped to his feet and laughed.

'Yah, he said, 'you two are young and foolish. Sure you know nothing about life. Said the man, "Eat, drink and be merry, for to-morrow we die." Come on, we'll go down to Carmody's.'

'No, I must go home,' said the Stranger, also rising. 'I don't feel very well.' He was very pale and weak and he trembled slightly, overwrought by his recent illness and his excitement.

'Damn my soul,' cried O'Daly tenderly, catching him by the shoulder, 'I didn't know you were seedy. Drink that brandy. There now. Kathleen, ye're the devil for talk. You ... fooh!' He glared at his daughter.

'I'm so sorry,' said Kathleen. 'Of course I didn't mean to irritate you. Please forgive me.'

The Stranger took her hand and laughed.

'Oh, that's all right,' he said. 'I'm quite all right, quite. It's only nervousness. I'm frightfully sorry.' But he had seen the softness in Kathleen's eyes and the blush that suffused her neck as she spoke, and it maddened him still more inwardly. He felt that she was superior to him, had more command over herself, was purer. 'I must go now,' he said. 'No, no, don't move, Mr. O'Daly. Good night.'

Kathleen began to apologize to him again at the door, but he laughed and bid her good night hurriedly. She watched him going down the path and then called out, 'Be sure to come again soon.'

'All right,' he called, 'thanks.' And then, walking hurriedly down the road, he said, 'Never. Never again. I'm lost. I'm not fit to associate with her. I'm accursed. What a wreck I have made of my life!'

Spring

1

WINTER died with a melancholy roar of all the elements. For three days storm-driven rain fell furiously on Inverara, while the exhausted sea writhed in the death agony of its winter madness. Then the sun rose in an arc of shimmering light south of the Head of Crom. It shot out its myriad tentacles over the sea and land. It sent out a heatless invigorating light. The sea danced, rippling, and hummed a tune like the sound of insects breathing on a weed-covered rock, as it tossed against the cliffs. Inverara, washed by the rain and torn by the wind, cracked in every pore noiselessly as it began to move. The dew on the crags glittered and then died, sucked into the sun. Each tuft of withered grass that had lain during the long winter between the crevices of the crags, bitten by the frost, shivered. Green sprouts began to crawl up through the withered ones. In the bare green plains above the beach at Coillnamhan the grasses began to wave their pointed heads spasmodically. Like blind men they clawed the air, seeking a way to the sun and warmth. The worms,

dizzy after their winter's sleep, their heads swaying
drunkenly on the coil of their bodies, squirmed in the
cold light. The birds chirped as they flitted hither and
thither trying to find a mate and a nesting-place. The
larks rose with the bleak dawn, stammering as they
leaped from the earth, as if their music, frozen by
winter, was being melted in their throats by the joyous
light. Their voices rang out clear and defiant as they
soared high over Inverara. The heralds of spring and
life, they sounded the reveille to the earth below.

'Spring has come. Up, you laggards. Your sleep is
o'er.' So whispered the wind, coming in fast, hissing
rushes from the sea. It was no gentle, languorous wind.
It was sharp and biting. It beat the earth with thin steel
rods. It throbbed with energy. It hardened the muscles.
It sent the blood rushing from the heart to the limbs. It
made the teeth chatter. It aroused passion. It was full of
cold lust. It poured into every crevice of the crags,
catching everything in its harsh grip. It poured into
every cabin to rouse the people. It made the horses
neigh and gallop, as it tore the shaggy winter hair from
their backs. It was the lashing wind of spring.

The back of the sea was covered with wrinkles as if
it were shrinking from the cold caress of the wind.
And, spurred by the wind, it struck the cliffs mighty
blows gently, like a giant who is building with heavy
instruments. It rolled banks of yellow and brown and
black seaweed to the beaches to fertilize the earth. Its
broad bosom was covered with low ridges, as it heaved
itself towards the land, driven by the wind, white thin
lines dividing green swathes of water. It hurried,
ceaselessly building on the ruins of winter. Its
never-ending sound carried all over Inverara, like the

panting breath of nature building spring. Every living thing in Inverara breathed its strong smell that was carried on the wind. It loosened stiff limbs and poured iron into blood that had thinned in winter.

Life, life, life, and the labour of strong hands in Inverara in spring. From dawn to dark the people hurried, excitedly opening the earth to sow. At dawn they came from their cabins, their noses shining with frost, slapping their lean hands under their armpits, their blue eyes hungry with energy. They ran through the smoking dew for their horses. From dawn to dark their horses trotted, neighing, their steel shoes ringing on the smooth stones. Through rain and driven sleet the people worked. Cows gave birth to calves, and the crooning of women milking in the evening mingled dreamily with the joyous carolling of the birds. Yellow lambs staggered by their mothers' sides as they made their first trembling journeys in life. Lean goats were hiding their newborn kids in the crevices among the crags. Everything moved hungrily for life. Even the grey limestone crags seemed to move as the sun sucked the dew from their backs. Smoke rose everywhere, as if nature perspired conceiving life.

The valley that lay beneath Rooruck, bound on the south by the ivy-covered low hill where the crags ended and on the north by the stretch of black, rocky, sandless beach, teemed with sounds of work. Each plot of land, bound by stone fences, was being tilled. Rotted seaweed, whitened by the rain, lay like a healing rash on the yellow grass, spread in winter. Heaps of fresh seaweed, glistening in the sun and sleet, were being dropped here and there from the horses' backs. Peasants, with their white frieze shirts hanging loose about their bodies, were cutting the earth with spades, covering the potato seeds that the women were spreading. Fierce sounds filled the air, men shouting, horses neighing, spades beating the earth, boys lashing donkeys with seaweed stems, sleet pattering against stone walls.

Spring did not come in a night. It did not emerge from winter like a shell from a cannon mouth. It came gradually. But to the Stranger it appeared to come in a flash, drear and ghastly. For a week after returning from his meeting with O'Daly's daughter he kept indoors, feverishly disputing with himself, unconscious of everything around him. Sitting silently by the fire, he argued with Kathleen O'Daly, defending his own cynicism against her piety, his own weakness against her fortitude. 'Bah,' he would say, 'she is a fool. Everything is dead. What is the use of virtue or ambition or God? They are all meaningless.' And yet he could not drive away her memory. Her memory aroused memories of his youth, sweet ambition, respectability, the regard of fellow beings, the solace of religion. She was the emblem of what he had left, of what he had thrust from him. He was conscious that he had gained nothing in exchange. And he clung to that nothing, that annihilation of life, as men cling to a worthless article for which they have paid dearly. 'She is a hypocrite,' he would say. He accused her of gross immoralities, but he shuddered at the thought as at a profanation of his mother. He tried to arouse obscene desires in his mind for her in order to break the spell of her personality, but in vain. He could not think of her as a woman in the flesh. She was almost a spirit. She was the personification of memories. And in revolt against this spell he lounged slothfully about the cabin, unshaved, unwashed, scowling, in order to drive himself farther down into the abyss of degradation where even memories of cleanliness could not reach him.

For that whole week he was never conscious of Little Mary or her husband. They moved about him without his seeing them. Red John obeyed the spring like an automaton. He obeyed it unconsciously like the grasses that were being thrust from the earth in spite of themselves. His weak will revolted against life that was a joyless burden to him, but the remorseless wind lashed him into action. He worked ceaselessly mending baskets, splicing ropes, manuring the two fields in which he was preparing to sow potatoes, cutting seeds. And all the while his passion for Little Mary, fanned by the lustful spirit of spring, maddened him. But her glance terrified him. He saw that she was lost to him. He would look from her to the Stranger sitting slothfully by the fire, and his eyes gleamed with hatred. Then they changed immediately and distended with fear. Drear phantoms pursued one another through his savage unreasoning mind that brought his breath from his lungs in gasps. So he worked furiously without purpose to keep himself from going mad. He sowed, caring nothing whether he should reap or not. He no longer raged against his fate. The people about him lost interest for him. He could understand nothing. There was a great want within him continually demanding satisfaction, and he was unable to satisfy it. He wanted his wife. The wind of spring lashed the marrows of his bones, urging him to satisfy that want. The crazy structure of his reason lurched dangerously.

He spoke to nobody and they shook their heads at him contemptuously, saying, 'What a boor of a fellow. It's avarice that makes him that way.' Nobody cared to find the cause of his melancholy, least of all his wife, Little Mary. Spring was in her blood too, but it was to her an elixir that made her shiver with love of life. She moved jauntily, with a springing step, swaying from the hips. Her eyes glittered mischievously. The dimples in her cheeks when she smiled were lost in a thousand creases. Her teeth when she bared them in a laugh shone like ivory. She used to look at the Stranger sitting moodily by the fire and smile to herself. 'Ha,' she would say, 'it is the beginning.' It seemed that a skittish imp had entered her soul that was gentle and sad in winter. That imp transformed her. Her beauty, that was sombre in winter like the beauty of a mist-clad mountain, was now maddening like the beauty of a fountain in which sunbeams are sparkling.

Then one morning the Stranger awoke from sleep, conscious of all the activity about him. Sounds reached him from all sides of people working. They had reached him every morning for the past week, but they had flitted past unheeded. His mind, busy with its controversies, did not grasp their meaning. As he dressed he heard the bleating of a sheep coming down the lane at the back of the cabin. He went to the window and looked out. A peasant woman was carrying a newborn lamb in her arms. Its body, yellow with the shine of birth, hung awkwardly across her breast, its long legs dangling, its large ears drooping. A little boy running by the woman's side kept stroking its head and skipped as he shouted, 'Tuirteen a'm, tuirteen a'm.' A sheep circled around bleating, a brier trailing from her haunch, her belly covered with hard pellets of earth that jingled as she ran. The woman held the lamb to the sheep's nose now and again to ease her fierce anxiety.

The Stranger felt a pain in his chest looking at the sight. It appeared to be the embodiment of life to him, of spring, of awakening energy. Then with it came all the other sounds of life. From the cabin door he could see the whiteshirted men working in the fields beneath the village. The perspiration shone on the horses' flanks as they galloped past him. Their dung smoked in the lane. The wind ran close to the earth with a whipping sound. He stood looking out motionless, as if amazed at the treachery of nature's return to life and activity. He felt as bitterly alone as the roué, when all his boon companions have suddenly deserted vice for a life of virtue. He stood looking out of the door for fully half an hour, unable to understand it.

Little Mary was preparing his breakfast in the kitchen behind him. He could hear her humming a song carelessly as she moved about. The sound of water gurgling from the spout of the kettle into the teapot appeared strange to him, as if he had never heard it before. He was afraid to turn around to look at her, lest she too might have changed in the night with the rest of the world about him.

'Your breakfast is ready,' she said.

He wheeled about and looked at her. She moved to the window without glancing at him and stood looking out dreamily, arranging a curl of hair on her right temple. He stood by his chair staring at her as if she had done him an injury. He tried to think of something to say to her. But he couldn't speak. Something

fermented within him that tied his tongue to his palate.
'Fuh!' he said at last, querulously, and banged the chair
against the ground. She shot him a coquettish glance
and went out. Then he heard her calling loudly to her
hens, 'Tiuc! tiuc! tiuc! come here to me, you darlings,'
as if she had completely forgotten all about him. But
she kept smiling to herself as she thought, 'Now I can
play with him.'

He gulped his breakfast, angry with himself. Then
he walked about the kitchen excitedly. He put on his
hat and coat to go for a walk, but he turned back from
the door and took off his coat again. Then he swore
when he realized that he wanted her. The memory of
Kathleen O'Daly came before his mind. He found
himself thinking religiously, he who was an atheist. 'It
would be a sin,' he said to himself, standing by his bed.
But the very thought aroused his passion the more.
Then he laughed aloud at the incongruity of his
thinking that such a thing could be sinful in the eyes of
a man who scoffed at the world, in the eyes of a man
who had ... well, done all the things that men do when
they cut adrift. He went into the kitchen and sat by the
fire waiting for her. Then she came in. He smiled at her,
but she never noticed him.

'Is it cold outside?' he said, wondering how he
should approach her.

'No,' she said carelessly, shrugging her shoulders.
'I'm going to the fields to spread seeds now. Would
you like to come and watch?'

'No, I would not,' he said angrily. 'The devil take the
seeds!' He put on his coat again and rushed out.

He wanted to go eastwards to Carmody's
public-house at Coillnamhan, but he found that he

could not leave Rooruck. He kept circling around the field in which Little Mary was working. He fashioned all kinds of excuses to pass by that field. When he came near it, he talked to the peasants in the neighbouring field, and passed on without speaking to her. And then, coming up again to the cabin, he cursed himself for an utter idiot. His pride was insulted by the fact that passion was gaining the mastery over him. His winter apathy was slipping away from him. In fact, before dinner he shaved himself and trimmed his beard. He felt the lack of flesh on his bones, and wished that he was in better condition and less repulsive physically. And all the while some skittish imp kept smirking within him, hiding from his accusing conscience. He felt a quickening of his pulse and a warmth in his blood. He was almost dizzy with that strange feeling of spring. And it was completely physical, overpowering the mind like wine. In fact, it formed a mind of its own, with a distinct philosophy and a moral code. That mind seemed to be not in the brain but somewhere around the heart and the bowels. It shut out the past and the future, and demanded immediate satisfaction of its desires. It was cold and biting like the wind. It was irresistible.

While Little Mary was preparing dinner for him he watched her breathlessly, struggling violently with himself. In her presence he felt ashamed, conscience stricken. But when she was leaving the cabin to take Red John's dinner to the field he caught her by the hand and looked into her eyes. She laughed and snatched away her hand. He swore. She stopped at the door and said in a rippling voice, 'I'm in a hurry.' Then she ran down the lane.

'Curse the woman,' he said, 'she's making a fool of me. All right. That finishes it. Good God, I was mad to think of a peasant woman. I'm becoming utterly degraded. I'm finished with women! They are the curse of life. There, she's been trying to tempt me. I'm glad I resisted her advances.' And he ate his dinner hungrily, quite satisfied with himself. Then he endeavoured to fall back into his slothful habits of winter. He sat by the fire smoking. But he couldn't rest. His hands and feet were fidgeting. He suggested all sorts of activities, a walk by the Hill of Fate, a visit to the old fort, a turn around the fields where the peasants were working, but none of these things satisfied him. All these places were connected with Little Mary, and he must avoid her. Finally, towards evening, he set out towards Coillnamhan. He told himself that his walk there was completely without purpose, but he sat on a fence above the beach, waiting. That was the road from the school to O'Daly's house. He kept watching the hill between him and the school. Kathleen O'Daly would come along that way.

Then he saw her coming over the hill talking to another man, a priest. He made a movement to jump from the fence, but he held back. 'Why should I run away from a woman?' he asked himself. He tried to calm himself and be indifferent as he waited until she came up. He could hear her laughing as she approached, but he wouldn't look in her direction. He was watching two seagulls on the beach quarrelling raucously over the carcass of a dogfish. Then he turned towards her suddenly and raised his hat as she was passing.

'Good evening, Miss O'Daly,' he said.

Kathleen stopped dead and made a startled gesture.

'Good gracious! Mr. O'Connor,' she said, 'you gave me a fright. I never saw you.' She had in fact seen him a long way off. 'Let me introduce you to our curate, Father Ronan – Mr. O'Connor, Father Ronan.'

The Stranger shook hands with the curate with an effort at cheerfulness, although he hated priests. He associated them in some peculiar way with all the things that had caused his ruin. The curate, a squat, heavily built, shabbily dressed man with a dark face and beautiful grey eyes, stammered something inaudibly and then smiled. He began to smile towards the Stranger, and finished smiling towards Kathleen. He was always shy of men, though quite at home with women. A most peculiar man, though a fine character, and absolutely sincere in his belief in his religion and mission. His body was that of a prize-fighter, but his eyes were those of a nun, and his manner corresponded with his eyes. He could look no man in the eyes, and he always blushed and fidgeted when talking. His face would darken suddenly, and he would grip his side as if he had a stitch in it. The Stranger misunderstood his embarrassment. 'He's in love with her,' he said to himself. 'The hypocrite!' Then he himself fell in beside Kathleen and began to talk cheerfully and nonchalantly. He would show the yokel of a priest that he was a man of the world. But his affected cynical bantering had no effect either on Kathleen or the priest. They both pitied him. They did not get irritated as he hoped they would. They merely raised their eyebrows and said a word now and again in agreement with the most bitterly cynical things he could say about the country and its religion. They parted almost in silence at the western end of the beach. As he shook hands with Kathleen she pressed his hand slightly and looked pityingly into his eyes.

'You must come to see us often,' she said; 'my father is always talking about you. Do please come.'

The curate tried to say something and then blushed and looked at Kathleen. The Stranger could catch the words 'interesting books.'

'Ah, yes,' said Kathleen, 'if you should like something to read, Father Ronan would be pleased – '

The Stranger interrupted her with a wave of his hand, and began to walk away.

'No,' he said, 'I prefer to be a primitive man. I have no wish to be converted.' And he walked on.

The roads parted at right angles. He walked hurriedly for a short distance, and then paused to tie his shoe-lace, which did not want to be tied. He undid it and then tied it again as he looked after the other couple. They were on the brow of the hill, going towards the village. Kathleen kept twitching her shoulders slightly as she walked, and held herself very straight, staring in front of her. A curl of hair waved from beneath her black round cap.

'You should try and save him,' the curate was saying. 'There is something on his soul.' And Kathleen smiled, glad to give that construction to her desires.

But the Stranger, watching them, thought they had forgotten all about him.

'They think I'm not fit to associate with them,' he thought. 'Wouldn't even argue with me. Very well. To hell with them. It's just the price of you, Fergus O'Connor.' And suddenly he laughed aloud, and drew his lower lip over his mouth. 'There's Little Mary, anyway,' he said. Going westwards the sharp wind cut into his marrows, and he felt the urge of spring fiercely. 'Hurrah!' he shouted, and threw his hat in the air. 'I wish I could commit some heinous crime to satisfy myself.'

He passed Red John riding on his pony near the cottage. Red John did not speak, but lashed his pony and passed at a flying gallop, his short legs swinging in opposite directions along the horse's flanks. The Stranger could hear him swear at his horse long after he passed out of sight.

'All right, you lout,' he muttered viciously; 'I'll make you a cuckold for your surliness.'

All feelings of refinement had left him now. Spring held him in a strong grip that crushed his conscience. He was like a primitive savage. He vaulted over the stone fence into the yard, and opened the door without pausing. Little Mary was laying his supper, her back turned towards him. Without looking around she moved to the fire and said:

'Did you pass Red John on your way?'

'Yes,' he said; 'where was he going?'

'Into Kilmurrage for a new spade. I don't suppose he will be back before morning. Whenever he gets a shilling he drinks it. He has my heart broken.' And she gazed at the fire mournfully in pretended woe.

But the Stranger saw the colour mounting in her cheeks, giving the lie to her words. He sat down to his supper in silence and toyed with the food, but he couldn't swallow anything. His heart was thumping wildly. He sat listening to the silence without for fully a minute. There was a long-drawn hissing from the west, of a wave receding over a pebbly beach. The sound like a command made him stand up. He had to move his chair, and the act irritated him. Then he moved swiftly to her and bent down over her shoulders until his cheek touched hers. He could feel her body trembling. With a sigh she turned around and fell into his arms.

It was dark when he threw himself on his bed. His head swam. His body seemed to be on fire, burning with the shame that seized him for having taken her. He writhed on the bed, murmuring, 'Christ! what possessed me to do it?' He felt that he had committed himself to her now. His surrender to his passion hurled him back again into the world. It appeared gross to him. He tried to laugh scornfully, but he couldn't. He repeated continually, 'I don't love her. I shouldn't have done it. She trusts me.' He was in agony when he recalled the look in her eyes as she lay in his arms. They were gentle, soft, trusting. He tore his hair and bit the bedclothes with his teeth. Then he lay still, and gradually his mind began to calm. Instead of being ashamed of himself he now became angry with Little Mary for having succumbed to him. But his anger was unreal, and he lay on his side, resting his head on his hand, staring at the wall, wondering what he should do now. Should he run away? Yes, he would run away. He got up and packed his clothes. Then he realized that he couldn't get a steamer to the mainland until the following day, and sat down again on his bed. He sat there for a long time thinking gloomily until he heard the door open and somebody stagger into the kitchen. He jumped to his feet and rubbed his eyes. It was broad daylight.

'Hey there! hey there!' came Red John's voice in a

thick whisper; 'is there nobody in this kip of a place?'
He kicked at a chair and upset it.

The Stranger went into the kitchen and asked him
what was the matter.

Red John, his clothes spattered with mud, and his
beard matted with porter froth, clung to the dresser
with his right hand.

'Ho! ho! there, my fine fellow,' he chuckled, 'so there
you are, you son of a loose woman. You spawn of a
dogfish. You –' He uttered a wild yell, and began to
tear his shirt from his back when Little Mary came
rushing at him from her room, and he dropped on his
knees in a trice. 'Don't strike! merciless woman,' he
whined; 'they wouldn't give me a spade. They
wouldn't open the shop to me, I tell you, so I had to
drink in Mulligan's while I sent a boy to look for one. I
declare by the cross of the Crucified One that I couldn't
get a spade. What's all this noise now about a spade?
Haven't I got a good spade already?' He kept babbling
as he crawled to the hearth and sat down glaring at the
two of them like a wild animal. Little Mary shrugged
her shoulders and said nothing.

'Good God, what sent me to this place?' thought the
Stranger. He became filled with such a violent disgust
at his sordid surroundings that he wanted to rush
away and leave them. But where should he go? He
stayed in his room all day trying to think out a plan.
Impossible! The very coldness of the air outside was a
barrier against going anywhere. He avoided Little
Mary's eyes. He never spoke to her. He wanted to go to
the O'Dalys and ask their advice. But how could he tell
them that he had seduced Red John's wife? And all day

he heard Red John shouting and screaming in the other room.

'They'll eat me alive,' he screamed; 'blue devils and little red ones with clay pipes in their mouths.' It was like being in hell, listening to the man's drunken babble.

'I wish a devil would choke him and be done with it,' he thought. He went into the kitchen for his supper and saw Little Mary calmly knitting by the fire as if nothing in the world troubled her. 'Huh!' he thought, 'she's an unnatural woman. Good God, she has ruined me,' forgetting her kindness to him in winter, and her love that made her give him herself.

He scowled at her fiercely, but she never looked. All day she was in a cloud of happiness that nothing could pierce. Since the night before, when she had abandoned herself to her love, she was unable to think of anything but the consummation of her womanhood. It was the beginning of life. If even it were the end of life, it had at least been worth while to have lived for those moments. Like an opiate her satisfied love made her insensible to her surroundings, even to the object of her love. Not a single shadow of gross conventions or cowardly morality darkened the cloud of her happiness. She was not tortured by the desire that civilized women have to demand a price for their affections by marriage or otherwise. She had given freely like nature. She received from nature the clean gift of satisfied womanhood.

But his own vanity and the philosophy of degenerate fools filled the Stranger with the wind of remorse. That night as he lay down to sleep he said to himself, 'I will keep aloof from the two of them. It is wrong for an educated man to lower himself to the level of peasants.' For a fortnight he did so. He roamed around Rooruck restlessly, speaking to nobody. He pretended to be quite at his ease in his gloomy solitude, but he was most unhappy. At night he slept well. He ate his meals with relish. He felt himself getting stronger every day, and his returning strength was detestable to him. It aroused his passion. It made him want to exercise his hands and his mind in doing something. Each day was a perpetual struggle between his resolution to be miserable and the urge of spring and returning strength urging him to love and activity.

'O God of the valiant deeds, what a ghoul of a fellow!' the peasants would say as he passed them in silence with a cold stare. The young women of the village, who were all out in the fields or on the shore, would glance at him giddily and say, 'Hist! why the hurry?' but he would take no notice of them. Then they would whisper loud enough for him to hear, 'He's not a man at all, I believe. They say he was badly wounded in the big war. What a pity!' And their jibes maddened him.

Those days Little Mary spent in trembling anxiety, afraid that he was lost to her. She would look at him, sometimes sadly and wearily, with wide-open eyes in which the hidden tears were glistening. Sometimes she looked at him with hatred in her eyes and her nostrils quivering because he scorned her. Each night she lay awake a long time thinking furiously of what she should do if he looked at her no more. She would listen savagely to the sea beating against the cliffs, and picture her own body washed away on its bosom. And then she would say, through her clenched teeth, as she clasped her throbbing throat, 'I will make him love me. I will, or I will kill him.' For her primitive soul was as merciless as nature itself. The tender growth of civilization had never taken root in her mind. Her love raged mightily. Like an ocean wave there was nothing either within her or without her to stay its progress. It must satisfy itself or shatter itself in death.

Then nature turned the Stranger towards her again. Nature routed his body from its winter apathy. It left his mind, which was not of nature but of civilization, wriggling in the clutches of his fantastic reasoning, but his body, nourished by the exhilarating breath of the sea and hardened by the wind, was drawn by an overpowering force to a mate. The most ferocious castigations prescribed by the Christian Church for the unsexing of its cherished saints would have been of no avail to silence the demands of nature in Rooruck in spring. That spring at Rooruck, when strong men live greedily every moment from the grey cold dawn to the mist-laden dusk! Life there is only to the strong and to the ruthless. Oh, strong, beautiful sea! Hunger-inspiring! Life-giving! Oh, the icy clasp of the wind, like the stern command of a proud father. Even when it numbs the limbs at dawn the heart throbs joyfully, loving life. So even though his weak mind remained helpless, his body grew daily fonder of life. Two personalities grew within him side by side. One embraced Little Mary and loved her bodily with the love of nature. The other hated her and kept hidden behind a gloomy silence. And she tried her utmost to gain access to those caverns where his Black Soul lurked.

'Talk to me,' she would say as they sat together in

the kitchen. 'Tell me about the places you have been, about the war, and all the strange countries you saw. Do tell me!' She was eager to learn what he knew of life, so that she could interest him by talking and make herself more attractive to him.

For many days he refused to talk, saying to her, 'What is the use of my talking to you, you would not understand me.' Then at last his loneliness became so oppressive that he had to speak. He talked furiously as he walked about the kitchen, forgetful of what he was saying or to whom he was speaking. He talked fiercely, like spring, of conquest, of great deeds. He felt, in the ecstatic pleasure of talking to some one, that he could achieve wonders.

She listened to him breathlessly. A new vista of happiness opened up before her eyes. Oh, to have words like those spoken to her! Her love that was before but the creation of her own fancy, now swelled within her torrentially as she realized that he had her respect. She fell in love with his mind that could conceive those words. How sweet they were, those fierce words, and the gleaming eyes through which the mind peeped and disappeared flashing, like sunbeams through a cloud. With her arms folded on her breast, and her head turned sideways to hear better, she sat rocking herself like a nun in a spiritual ecstasy.

But he felt none of her happiness. He suddenly stopped talking, and without casting a glance at her went out. A terrible weariness seized him. He always felt that discontent when he had talked a great deal, as if there were something he wanted to do and couldn't do. Night was falling as he walked down the village towards the beach. A bitter wind blew fitfully, almost drowned by a dirty grey mist that seemed to be rolling up before it the rays of the sinking sun. It was as if the sun, like a sick man recovering from a long illness, were giving up its feeble attempt to warm the earth and the dregs of winter were putting it to flight. Through the mist he could see dim grey forms coming towards him, peasants coming wearily homewards after their day's work, with spades on their shoulders. They were talking idly and laughing. They talked of women. There was a lewd ferocity in their tired voices. Now and again one of them would yell and scrape his spade along the stone fence as if seized by a drunken frenzy. In spite of himself he felt his blood rush hotly at their remarks and they disgusted him.

'Good God,' he thought, 'how coarse I am becoming! I, an educated man!' But his body revolted against this priggishness of his mind. Said spring within him: 'You know very well educated men are far worse than these poor peasants in matters of the kind, but they are too cowardly to express them only. Vice is born of repression.' 'That's right,' he thought, and suddenly he became aware that the reason he had kept away from Little Mary for the past fortnight was because she had given herself to him. And he had thought Kathleen O'Daly superior to Little Mary. Why? Obviously because she was better dressed, respectable, and had been to a university. Fancy setting a woman like that above Little Mary, a shallow conceited woman, just like the artificial unsexed ladies who haunt the suburbs of large cities, full of sham intellectual vanities, the mainstay of society doctors, spiritualists, psychoanalysts, and freak writers. He recounted all Little Mary had done for him in winter when he was ill.

He felt the warm fragrance of her body lying within his arms. He saw the wild love-light in her half-closed eyes turned up to his, and he shuddered, hating himself for having slighted her in his mind. But even as he did so his morose intellect sardonically recalled the wondrous music of Kathleen's violin, the refined hands, the ripple of the curls on her cheeks. He struck his forehead heavily and swore. The blow brought him back to his senses, and he stopped with a start and looked about him.

He found himself standing half-way out on the Jagged Reef, absolutely alone in the dark night. He could hear the low rumbling of the sea in front, coming up to him through the mist. The rocks at his feet were covered with yellow sea moss, slippery and glistening. White froth oozed from it, where his feet rested. Birds ran screaming along the rocks. He could just see their long, bright, red legs. Their bodies, the colour of the grey mist, were invisible. Cormorants, flying close to the ground, their gullets heavy with the day's fishing, side-stepped with a whizzing sound as they passed him. And overhead there was nothing visible but the black fat belly of the mist. The sharp biting wind made him shiver. 'Christ,' he said, 'what a night!' Oppressed by nature that was black as his own soul, he began to walk out hurriedly towards the sea, pretending to himself that he could endure life no longer, and that he was going to drown himself. The tide was nearly at a low ebb, and he seemed to have been walking for hours before the mighty vastness loomed up suddenly at him out of the mist. Its vast, dark, moving face leered. Aghast at the thought of jumping into the belly of such an appalling monster, he wheeled about sharply and slipped on the moss. He fell on his knees in a pool. His teeth began to chatter. He scrambled to his feet and ran back madly over the rocks. He stumbled among the pools. He thought an army of ghosts surrounded him. He felt sure that a huge animal was hurtling along behind him trying to catch him by the heels. When he reached the cabin he sighed with delight and broke into a walk. He was perspiring. He looked around cautiously lest anybody should have seen his hurried flight, and then began to whistle nonchalantly and swing his arms as he walked towards the cabin. He kept shaking his head and saying to himself, 'By God, never again will I slight Little Mary.' He wanted her to comfort him, so he persuaded himself that he was a fine fellow and loved her.

He saw two great mastiffs standing outside Red John's door, wagging their tails and smelling each other's noses. Red John's cur was lying on its back at their feet, whining and shivering when the mastiffs sniffed at it contemptuously. He recognized the dogs as O'Daly's, and jumped over the gate, eagerly chuckling to himself. 'Jove, I'll have a great talk with him.' The two mastiffs made a snarling rush at him. He was always afraid of dogs, but he joyously kicked at them as if the great hairy things with jagged fangs were timid sheep. He opened the door and entered the kitchen.

'How are you, Mr. O'Daly? Delighted to see you.'

O'Daly made a noise as if he were urging on a horse, as he turned around on the stool in front of the fire. With one hand stroking his beard and the other hand on his right knee, he looked at the Stranger with his peculiar ferocious look that never inspired fear or embarrassment, but love for the strange old fellow.

'Well,' he said, shaking his head like a horse, 'you are a queer person. Upon my soul, you are as unsociable as an Englishman. Why don't you come to see the people? Sit down and tell us what devilment you've been up to. Sit down here and talk to the people.'

'Wait until I change my clothes,' said the Stranger, laughing; 'I'm wet to the neck.' He went into his room.

'How are you getting on with your sowing, Red John?' said O'Daly, taking out his pipe and looking from Red John and Little Mary, who sat in opposite corners, back and forth, fiercely as if he were interrogating them at the Petty Sessions in his capacity as a magistrate.

Red John drew his legs up under him and sniffed. 'Oh, well enough, well enough,' he said with a sigh.

'My soul from the devil,' cried O'Daly, 'what a miserable fellow you are. You're the most' – he pulled at his pipe – 'miserable fellow I ever met. So you are.' He cracked his fingers, wagged his head, and blew clouds of tobacco smoke from his mouth. 'My soul from the devil, but you have the most beautiful woman in Inverara, and yet you are a miserable fellow. How do you explain it? What do you say about it, my good woman?' He began to talk to Little Mary, subtly flattering her, until she almost cried with laughter and enjoyment, while Red John's forehead twitched as he looked from one to the other of them. He would look at Little Mary's beautiful face and flashing eyes and say to himself, 'My woman, eh? May the devil rape her.' Then he would look at O'Daly with hatred. He hated him because he was big and strong, and was able to talk freely to women. His eyes would roam over

O'Daly's brown patched suit that hung loosely about
his lean body, and he imagined that even the stuff of
the cloth was a living enemy. The game bag that hung
on O'Daly's shoulder assumed the properties of an
enemy. It was associated with the things that he never
knew, that he never possessed. Even the blood-stained
head of a curlew that protruded from a hole in the side
of the bag leered at him. It said, 'There you are, you
miserable peasant, you never could kill a curlew. You
are a poor oppressed wretch. You are a worm. You are
only fit to be kicked like a cur.' And the gun that lay on
the ground beside O'Daly, its barrel gleaming in the
firelight, seemed to threaten him with instant death if
he dared to lift a finger in order to assert his manhood.
As he sat in his corner his soul shrank to a trembling
point in his breast. The whole range of his
understanding cowered within that point in awe of
everything that moved about him. Not a solitary being,
not even a dog or a bird, watched with him in
sympathy. He was alone, without even the knowledge
of a God to comfort him. His reason was slowly dying
like a plant suiddenly stricken with drought under a
scorching sun. He sat still without thought, lest a
movement or a thought would betray his presence to
all these enemies that were eager to overwhelm him.
Slowly, fearfully, his soul fled backwards, dragging his
body with it into the vast unconscious emptiness of the
primeval life from which his ancestors had arisen. For
in Rooruck in spring life is only to the strong and the
ruthless.

The Stranger, dressing in his room, heard Little
Mary laughing merrily in response to O'Daly's
bantering, and he became madly jealous of her. He was

jealous not because he suspected that she did not love him – he took that for granted – but because she could laugh with another man. 'Nonsense,' he said to himself, 'O'Daly is an old man, and I don't love her anyway. What does it matter to me what she'does?' But he was furious, nevertheless. Every time she laughed, the ringing sound with a ripple in the middle of it, as if it caught in her throat, struck at his chest like the flat base of a hammer. He finished dressing and sat on his bed pettishly, saying to himself that he wouldn't go into the kitchen. Sitting there he discovered that he had never been jealous of any other woman in his life, and he decided that he must be becoming very weak-minded. 'It's this miserable existence that's –'

Just then O'Daly shouted to him.

'Oh, lawdy, lawdy dah! you take as long to dress as a woman.'

He laughed with pretended gaiety and strolled into the kitchen. He took a seat away from the fire so as to remain hidden from the light.

O'Daly eyed him up and down appraisingly.

'Begob, yer putting on flesh,' he said. 'Now, what d'ye think o' that. We'll soon make a man of ye. And sure yer father, Lord have mercy on him, was a fine man ... as good as the best.'

The Stranger shot a sharp glance at Little Mary and saw her smiling happily. He fumed and turned to O'Daly with a smile. He felt himself intensely flattered by O'Daly's remarking his returning strength. He was, after all, a strong man. Fancy a strong man concerning himself about a miserable woman! Yes, he would put her out of his head.

'I met your daughter Kathleen the other day,' he said, laughing; 'I am afraid she is trying to convert me.'

'Upon my soul, she will before she finishes, although she made a poor job of myself. Mind ye, don't fall in love with her. They all do. Although in my time we looked for a different kind. When I was young –'

The Stranger heard Little Mary make a movement, and forgot O'Daly immediately. His first impulse was joy at the success of his effort to make her jealous. Then immediately he despised himself for his meanness. She was smiling weakly at the fire, but her throat was throbbing, and the fingers of her right hand tapped her knee restlessly. Then she rose hastily and went into her room. She thought she would never get across the floor to her room. She threw herself face downwards on her bed and burst into tears.

'So he is in love with Kathleen O'Daly,' she gasped; 'that skimpy girl, that empty-headed doll! Oh, if I had her head between my hands!' Then she puckered up her lips and swept her hair back tightly from her forehead with her right hand. Her wet eyes hardened as she tried to arouse hatred against the Stranger. He had talked of Kathleen purposely to hurt her. She knew he had. She tried to persuade herself that she hated him and despised him, and did not want him any more. But then, as soon as she imagined life without him, she was seized with horror. Her mind, like a butterfly flitting among barren flowers, rushed terror-stricken from one thing to another trying to attach itself to some interest, but in vain. A black shroud descended on everything with a jeering rush as soon as she told herself that she didn't want him. And a flood of tears gushed afresh from her eyes in her misery. Then, sobbing, she dried her eyes, her jealousy washed out by her tears. 'No, no, I love him, whatever he does,' she panted. 'What else have I got?' And she began to beseech heaven, the sea and Crom Dubh to blast everybody that ever bore the name of O'Daly. She poured out a torrent of mad words endlessly, until she had to stop breathlessly. Then she was satisfied.

The Stranger, endeavouring to listen cheerfully to O'Daly's conversation, knew that she was weeping in her room, and he felt intensely ashamed of himself He longed to be able to go into the room to her and take her in his arms. But he felt Red John's red eyes piercing his right cheek. They were like the eyes of a she-wolf whose cubs are stolen. Yet he laughed in response to O'Daly's jokes. And his ability to laugh in such a situation made him feel that he was a cur. He wanted to get up and strike somebody. He was afraid of O'Daly, so he turned his wrath against Red John because he knew he was weaker than himself. He looked at him savagely. Red John, who had been looking at him malignantly, lowered his eyes and began to fidget with the fire. Then he rose and stretched himself with a foolish grin.

'I must go and see has Long Bartly got a pitchfork to lend me,' he muttered, and slunk out of the cabin. But he didn't go to Long Bartly's. He crossed up over the crags to where his black sheep were grazing on the cliff top and kept driving them up and down the crags all night. 'Hist!' he would say, throwing a pebble at them. 'Let the fairies take you. What good are you to me? May the maggots eat you. I am eaten myself by the devils.' And he would laugh like a child.

When Red John had gone out, O'Daly bent over

close to the Stranger and whispered, 'Something the matter with that fellow. How do they get on together?' nodding his head towards the room where Little Mary was.

'Oh, all right,' said the Stranger. 'Why?'

O'Daly looked at him curiously and then looked towards the fire, winking an eye.

'She is a beautiful woman. You had better take care of yourself.'

'Why?' said the Stranger again, irritably.

'Oh, nothing,' whispered O'Daly; 'women are the very devil.'

'Oh, rot!' said the Stranger, 'I'm a man of the world.'

'Hm, hm,' said O'Daly; 'it's funny how young men always think they're wiser than their fathers. Oh, well, I must be going. Good night, my good woman.'

Little Mary saw him to the door, begging him to stay longer and hoping in her heart that an evil demon would 'cast the light of the morning sun on his rotting corpse.' The Stranger walked down the road with him. They walked in silence for a while. Then O'Daly said: 'I pity that poor woman. Begob, it hurts my soul to see a beautiful horse hurt or a beautiful woman living in poverty. The cruel injustice of the world.'

O'Daly, who, like most Irishmen of his type, had no sense of justice whatever, felt that at that moment he would give a fortune to get Little Mary out of her miserable surroundings. Yet he would have whipped her with pleasure and with equal sincerity and feeling of justice had a birthmark on her face irritated him. They say that he once, at the same sitting of the Parish Court in Kilmurrage, acquitted a man for opening a neighbour's skull in a fit of anger, and sentenced

another man to a month's hard labour for tying a sharp
cord around an old goat's thigh. His type is almost
extinct to-day in the country, which does not
appreciate the impulsive strength of the iron men of
old who were so close to merciless unjust nature.

Suddenly O'Daly stopped in the road and laid his
hand on the Stranger's shoulder.

'Damn it, man,' he said, 'I don't like to see you
pining away here, wasting your life. It's no place for a
young man. I wouldn't mind, but your father was one
of the old tribe, one of ourselves. I know ye got good
blood in you. Mind, I'm not pokin' my old nose, but if
there's anything I could do ... There now, what the hell
am I talking about?' And he began to curse loudly and
gruffly in order to hide his sudden exposure of what he
considered a disgraceful show of sentiment. The
Stranger kicked the road and said nothing. 'Hell to my
soul,' said O'Daly, catching his hand; 'come over any
time you've nothing to do and have a bottle with me.
Don't be too proud to visit an old man. Now good
night, and God bless ye, my son.' Then he stalked
down the road cursing himself for having taken an
interest in that 'good-for-nothing weakling; how in the
hell they breed them I don't know.'

The Stranger stood looking after him, clenching his
fist, grateful to him for his sympathy and at the same
time cursing him for having attempted to do him a
favour. He heard a small boy coming up the road
riding a donkey, and O'Daly stopped to talk to him.

'Oh, boys, oh, boys, where did you get that elegant
donkey?'

The Stranger turned sharply on his heel and walked
back to the cabin. 'Yeah, he forgot all about me

immediately,' he muttered angrily; 'nobody cares a damn about me.'

Through the thick darkness stray lights flickered here and there about him in the windows of the cabins. They were little sickly red scars on the black face of the night. One would heave up towards him glimmering, as if the night swayed, and then retreat again. Or was it his mind that swayed, endeavouring to find an exit from the conflicting suggestions that urged him to do this and to do that? O'Daly's words, 'you are wasting your life,' tumbled around in his brain, assuming strange formations as the words mixed, 'are you wasting your life,' 'life wasting you are,' in every conceivable way. He shrank from those words, and then pointing his finger at the sky he traced the words, 'I will waste my life as I think fit.' But that seemed to be childish. And his mind swayed again as suddenly something within said, 'Why bother about your life? There is Little Mary in there. Forget the world.' And he went into the cabin.

She was sitting by the fire rocking herself as he entered. She jumped up with an eager gleam in her eyes as she looked at him, but she immediately suppressed that look and stared coolly as she set a chair for him in front of the fire. Then she sat in the corner again, nervously arranging her shawl closely about her neck. He looked at her, feeling vexed with himself for having injured her, and with her for being the cause of his feeling vexed, for being a selfish fellow, like most men, he always took care to cast the blame for his meanness on other shoulders. His nerves began to strain at the silence and his lips twitched. One moment they twitched trying to hold back an onrush of apologies, at the very next moment trying to hold back an outburst of anger. In his anger he would say to himself, 'What right has she to be jealous of Kathleen O'Daly? It was her own fault if I am under an obligation to her.' Then when he looked at her sad beautiful face he grew tender. He would make a motion to reach out his hand to her and then draw back shuddering and put his hand over his mouth. At last he jumped to his feet and cried, 'Oh, damn this business, it will drive me mad.' He stood looking stupidly at the fire with his hands in his pockets. Unable to restrain herself any longer, she uttered a low cry, and jumping up threw her arms about his neck. But somehow her touch hardened him. He unbound her arms, and holding her by the shoulders looked into her eyes with set lips. She looked at him wearily. The sadness in her eyes pained his heart physically. He felt a desperate longing to kiss her and say sweet things to her. Yet something held him back, and he kept looking at her with hard eyes. Then Little Mary, her eyes staring with fright at his look, her bosom heaving with unborn sobs, rushed from his arms. She staggered to her stool and fell in a heap face downwards on it, bursting into tears. Then that something that held him back vanished with a snap and he fell on his knees beside her. He kissed her eyes, her lips, her ears, her forehead, her throat, her hands. He rubbed his hands through her hair, and pressing his cheek against hers, mumbled almost inaudibly, 'I love you, I love you.' Her sobs stopped suddenly, and she strained her ears excitedly, scarcely able to believe the words that she had hardly even dared to hope for. Slowly she raised her eyes to his face, and a low gurgling sound began to rise from her breast louder and louder, until it rushed from her lips almost with a scream, a sound that might be a scream of pain or of intense joy. Covering her eyes with her hands she nestled her head against his breast. With his chin resting on her head he knew that he loved her and he wondered fearfully what was going to be the outcome. Even love filled his Black Soul with fear.

And Little Mary, when he had gone to bed, sat by the fire kissing the places on her hands where his lips had rested.

2

AT Rooruck spring does not die. Like a river seeking the ocean, it gathered strength and beauty each day from its staggering frozen birth until it passed majestically into the luxuriant bosom of summer. Rooruck changed hour by hour, minute by minute, with each rush of the wind, each westward leap of the sun, each thud of the sea against its cliffs. The hungry black earth grew green with dewy grass. Sharp-pointed buds edged their way timorously through the hard soil of the tilled fields. The wind and rain descended softly on the crags and fields, whispering to the life that was coming from the womb of the earth. The air was fragrant with a sense of joy. It was like hearing good news of a loved one. Lambs frisked in the fields among the crags above the village, their growing wool already hanging from their sides in zigzag ringlets. Calves were rushing about stupidly, their tails in the air. The people began to laugh and look about them happily, their crops sown. They had already eaten eggs in homage to Crom for all the lives that had been born to them, from their sheep and cattle, on the day that Christians call Easter Sunday. One could almost hear nature clashing cymbals, urging life to grow. Beautiful, hard, grey spring life at Rooruck that swelled the chest and put steel into the eye and a warlike song in the throat. Full-grown spring at Rooruck that robbed men of fear and weakness.

Little Mary was as happy as the lark that rose each morning to sing from her grassy nest in the clover field beneath the cabin, where those furry-headed young larks were hugging one another. Now everything was plain to her. She could see the expanse of the future rolling itself out before her, and always she and her lover walked hand in hand across it. Every other year at the end of spring she had set a goose to hatch. But that year she did not. She had already cut herself adrift. She was waiting eagerly for her lover to say 'come,' waiting to fly with him over the sea. When they embraced she would look in his eyes and say, 'I wish we were together away from everybody.' And he would say, 'So do I, dearest,' and then bite his lips, for he feared that final step that would make him hers.

Nature tugged at his heart, urging him to be a man and take her with him out into the world, but his intellect refused to move in response to nature. 'How could I support her?' it would say. And then, 'What the hell do I want her for, anyway? I'm not going back into the world for anybody.' And his fear of having to go back to the struggle of life kept him in torment, preventing him from loving her. Every time he embraced her, the thought was constantly in his mind that she was trying to use him for her own purposes, selfishly. He told himself repeatedly that life did not interest him, and yet he felt the urge to do something growing daily more intense. The satisfied happy look on the faces of the peasants who had sown their crops maddened him. He felt like a soldier who is straggling behind a victorious army, unable to reach the conquered capital with them because he has led a debauched life. He felt everybody despised him, and that made him long still more to pretend indifference.

Then Bartly the son of Black Peter got married to a woman from Coillnamhan. Horses galloped madly from Rooruck to the church at Coillnamhan. Then they galloped back again, the bridegroom leading, with the bride riding pillion. The whole village gathered in Bartly's cabin and prepared to spend that day and the following night carousing, in celebration of the mating. Two men went around all the cabins in the village with a jar of whisky, forcing everybody to drink to the health of the newly wedded couple. Then everybody who had not been to the church drank a glass, saying, 'May their seed prosper,' and went to the wedding. Red John and Little Mary went. The Stranger, seeing Little Mary going to mix with the peasants, eager for the music and dancing, felt madly jealous and grew disgusted with her. It was as if he had seen a civilized savage woman eat human flesh in a moment of abandonment. At least he told himself that it was disgust, but he really felt vexed with her for being able to enjoy simple things from which he himself was cut off by his Black Soul and his foolish belief in his own importance. He waited alone in the cabin, listening to the distant sounds of merrymaking, and pretended that he was indifferent, but he could not feel indifferent. He kept wondering whether she was dancing with somebody else or whether she would smile into some other man's eyes and allow them to squeeze her waist.

Towards evening Little Mary came back to give him his supper. He saw her eyes gleaming with pleasure and her cheeks flushed with dancing and he was enraged with her. So he pretended to be indifferent. She noticed his jealousy and felt glad, because it showed her that he loved her.

'Do come down with me,' she said, clinging to him, 'the people won't like it if you don't come.'

'Oh, to hell with the yokels,' he said, 'I'm going in to O'Daly's and have somebody to talk to. What do I want with a lot of stupid savages?'

Then he ate his supper eagerly, with a great show of nonchalance, and went out.

Little Mary tore off the trinkets that she had donned so gaily that morning and sat by her bed, moaning, 'Now what have I done, now what have I done?'

He walked southwards from the village across the crags until he reached the cliffs. Then he turned eastwards towards the highest cliff, whose summit was crowned by the old fort that prehistoric warriors had built. He reached it. He passed through the two outer walls and then through the massive stone gate that led into the circular level greensward that was the fort itself. He stood still; there was perfect silence within the tremendous walls, in that circular bare patch of whitened grass, trodden by savage warriors three thousand years before. Four yards in front of him, the cliff dropped three hundred feet to a vast expanse of blue sea. 'Ah,' he said, and he felt strong and confident as if all the hosts that had ever looked out over that sea were beside him, defending him with their shields. He felt like a monk who sits in a vast empty cathedral communing with his god. He mounted the ramparts and lay on his belly along the broad wall of the fort looking out over Inverara. There were pale green streaks of light from the setting sun on the crags that sank in terraces from east and west and south to the broad grassy valley of Coillnamhan. The sea between Inverara and the blue mainland had a million dimples on its smooth face, kisses from the departing sun. The wide strip of sandy beach beneath Coillnamhan shone white, like the reflection of the moon at night in a tropical sea. White sheep, followed by their frisking lambs, wandered about the crags. Women in red petticoats crossed here and there with cans to milk their cows. The cows lowed. A pattering sound came from afar of somebody knocking a heap of smooth stones and a horse whinnied near there, eager for her evening drink of water perhaps. He gazed in silence, drinking in the beauty of nature. He wanted to embrace it, to hold it to his breast. Nature seemed to say, 'See how beautiful is the world. Fool. You despise peasants, do you? You think you are an intellectual? I'll tell you what you are. You are a charlatan. Go back now to the woman that loves you and enjoy life. It is good, but only to those who prefer truth to cheap cynicism and intellectual piffle.' And the ghosts of dead warriors seemed to clash their battle-axes silently on their shields and murmur, 'Aye, that is truth.' And the crags and the sea and the sand and the green valley winking under the parting embrace of the sinking sun seemed to sigh and say, 'Aye, peace and strength are only to those who can love beauty and truth. Beauty and truth are life. Life comes from our womb. Nestle close to us, my child. You will get lost in those clouds of vaporous intellectuality.'

And his Black Soul scowled at the accusing voice of nature. It said, 'Intellect is above nature. I am above the common herd, these peasants of Rooruck. What purpose is there in being happy or in trying to believe anything? What do I want to tussle with the ignorant mob for?' Then a great dark shadow passed westward from Kilmillick over the land and sea and blotted out the sun. A chill breeze began to blow. Shivering and depressed he descended from the ramparts and began to walk hurriedly down the slope towards Coillnamhan to O'Daly's house. He was obeying the voice of his Black Soul. It was the most satisfying voice to his vanity. So it is easier to scoff at life than to give a child an apple. But scoffing, though sweet, leaves a sour taste in the mouth, and a child's smile lives a long time in the memory.

The dark shadow had thickened into night before he reached the village. But he had ceased to notice anything about him. He was deliberately trying to persuade himself that he loved Kathleen O'Daly, that she was his equal in intellect, that her presence made him happy, that she had an elevating effect on his mind, and that Little Mary had a demoralizing effect on him.

'That kind of woman would turn me into a yokel. She would kill all refinement in me. I must pull myself together.' Then he knocked at the door of the cottage.

O'Daly opened the door to him and asked him to step inside in a whisper. He led him into the kitchen on tiptoe.

'There's a crowd o' them in there,' he whispered,

gripping the Stranger's right arm convulsively. 'Take this chair. That old woman of a curate and another priest from Dublin, full of nonsense about Republicanism, and a young woman with a face like the spine of a tinker's ass, relation o' the curate's, says she, "We need to enthuse the growing generation with a passion for pure ideals, and a clean unselfish moral life,"' and O'Daly tried to imitate the voice of a robin whose nest has been robbed. 'They're in there in the sitting-room,' he continued, breathing heavily as he filled an extra glass from a bottle that lay on the kitchen table. Then he handed the glass to the Stranger and sank into a bamboo arm-chair that cracked under his weight. 'I stuck it for an hour. Couldn't stand em any longer.' He had obviously made an attempt to 'stand it,' for he was wearing a starched shirt-front and a fairly new black suit. But the stiff narrow base of the shirt-front was sticking out over his waistcoat that was unbuttoned. He had torn off his tie, and the collar-stud was hanging loose at his throat. His face was as red as a beetroot with his exertions. The poor man would have liked very much to stay in the sitting-room and poke blasphemous fun at the priests and the young lady with the face like a tinker's ass's spine, but his daughter's stare told him that he was a 'disgrace,' so he had to retire. He was, after all, though 'an Irish gentleman who feared neither man nor devil,' as he said himself, afraid of his daughter and dependent on her. So he pretended that he really disliked the company and despised it. 'It's funny,' he said, filling himself a fresh glass of whisky, 'but the only people I feel like talking to are the peasants. They're more human than these bastards that pretend to know everything, and know nothing. Eh? Isn't that right?'

'Absolutely,' said the Stranger, swallowing his whisky. 'I quite agree with you,' he repeated with gusto, though an hour before he had told himself exactly the opposite. 'I feel as if I never wanted to leave Rooruck again.'

'Proper order,' said O'Daly, and he swallowed another glass. 'By God, this talk about pure ideals gives me the colic. None o' that in my time. Fellahs'd be ashamed to talk like that. May the devil swallow them and their ideals. Begob, yer a poor drinker. Hold yer glass over here. Woa, I'm spilling it, "the precious fluid," as old Father Mulligan used to say, God rest his soul.'

Now and again a subdued laugh came to them from the sitting-room as they drank. O'Daly, already half-drunk, had forgotten all about the party in the sitting-room, but the Stranger listened to every sound eagerly. It was as if he was eavesdropping on the civilized life that he once knew. He had forgotten about his pretended love for Kathleen. She again took her proper position in his mind, merely as a symbol of the life after which he hankered. And as usual, when he was listening to the voice of civilization, he told himself that he didn't want it. In fact, he pitied O'Daly, who was forced to live in such surroundings, and he kept drinking eagerly. Then the guests went away.

Kathleen came into the kitchen looking for her father. She was about to begin to scold him when she saw the Stranger and she stopped short.

'Hallo! my treasure,' said O'Daly, 'ye got-eh-rid of them at last.'

Kathleen stared at the two of them blinking with drunkenness, and then she turned on her heel and went out.

'Huh!' said O'Daly. Then he laughed and fell asleep in his chair.

The Stranger jumped to his feet and ran into the hall, shouting, 'Miss O'Daly, Miss O'Daly.'

'Yes,' she said sharply, coming up to him in the hall.

Under the influence of the whisky he felt quite brave and gallant.

'I hope I have done nothing to irritate you,' he said; 'I can assure you that –'

'Oh, it's quite all right,' she said coldly; 'I don't like to see men make beasts of themselves in my presence. Good night,' and she walked into the sitting-room.

'Oh, good Lord, what a razor tongue!' he murmured, going down the road. 'Now I see what she's like. My word, wasn't I lucky to have found her out. I bet Little Mary is as bad. But they won't catch me. I'm going to live my life freely.' Then he felt sure that all the women in the world were engaged in a conspiracy to trap him. He thrust out his chest and drew deep breaths and swung his arms, very proud of himself. He felt his muscles as he walked along and patted his thighs. His body was strong and supple after the wind of spring, good food and healthy living. His bodily strength made him feel independent and selfish. But on the top of these discoveries he suddenly felt a desire for Kathleen and he stopped in the road, vexed with himself.

'I'm becoming coarse,' he muttered disgustedly. 'After all, my only hope is to be faithful to Little Mary if I want to keep straight.' He was passing the Monks'

Well, where all the ghosts were seen. A stream ran across the road. They said that if a sinner stepped in the stream that the devils would devour him immediately. He stopped, looking at the dark rivulet. 'Wait now,' he said, 'I'll see whether I'm a sinner or not,' and he waded through it. Nothing happened, and he walked on quite cheered.

The guests were returning home noisily from Bartly's wedding as he passed through Rooruck. Men were singing songs and quarrelling. He vaulted over the fence into Red John's yard, and then he heard screams coming from the cabin. He stood still, looking at the curtained kitchen window where a candle was flickering. Then he heard Red John yell and a banging sound followed the yell, as of something being hurled against the door. Then Little Mary's shriek reached him. He rushed to the door and tried to open it. It was bolted on the inside.

'Hey there, hey there, open the door,' he shouted.

There was a moment's silence and then Little Mary screamed 'Help, help!'

He thrust his shoulder against the door. The wooden bolt smashed, the door swung open with a bang and he stumbled into the kitchen.

For a few moments he was dazed by the light and the excitement. Then he saw Red John standing near the fire, clothed only in his trousers and a strip of his woollen shirt on his right shoulder. There was froth on his red beard. He grinned savagely and gripped a tongs in his left hand. Little Mary was crouching in the corner by the back door, barefooted, with a red frieze petticoat thrown over her shift about her shoulders. Her teeth chattered with fright and shame.

Red John had come back from the wedding mad with whisky, and had attempted to embrace her. He sat by the fire mumbling that he would no longer let her treat him like a dog, trying to screw up his courage to take her. At one moment he feared her strength. At the next moment he forgot everything in his passion. Then he went into her room. She was asleep. He rushed to the bed and seized her. She jumped up with a scream and clawed at him. He drew back snarling. But when she saw his face, her strength and courage deserted her. Catching up her petticoat she fled into the kitchen. Seeing that she was afraid of him he pursued her and caught her in his arms as she was entering the Stranger's room. They struggled. She tore at his clothes and beard, while he tried to embrace her, growling like a dog. Then she broke from him and he fell on his back on the floor. She crouched at the back door, unable to escape in her terror. He got to his feet and hurled a sod of turf at her. Then he had grabbed the tongs from the hearth, when the Stranger came to the door.

The Stranger and he looked at one another in silence. They both trembled with passion, yet each feared the other. The Stranger felt that he was guilty of having stolen Red John's wife, and on the other hand felt that he must defend Little Mary. Red John was afraid that he had committed a crime by assaulting his wife, and yet he was enraged against the Stranger, whom he suspected of having seduced her. So they stood facing one another, each afraid to attack. They each tried to terrify the other. They curled up their lips. They expanded their chests and clenched their fists. They stepped about the floor threatening one another with their heads. Then the Stranger suddenly realized that the situation was ludicrous. He told himself that he was afraid of Red John and that he was in the wrong. Red John saw him hesitate and rushed at him. Then the Stranger forgot his reasoning, and shot out his hands to preserve himself. He was just in time to prevent the tongs from smashing his skull. Then he closed with Red John. Their faces were close together as they strained against each other. Then Red John thrust his head forward and tried to grip the Stranger's throat with his teeth. He missed the throat and tore at the coat lapel. Letting go his hands from the Stranger's waist he gripped at the throat like a dog. Then the Stranger, terrified into an equal fury, swung out blindly with both hands at Red John's head. Red John began to scream with pain. Gradually he let go his hold and then tried to stagger away. Another blow sent him down to the floor in a heap. 'Let me alone, let me alone,' he gasped, 'don't kill me, I didn't mean any-uh-harm to anybody.' And the Stranger, feeling disgusted with himself for having hurt the poor fellow after stealing his wife, staggered to a stool in the hearth corner, and hiding his face in his hands he wept.

He fell into a kind of thoughtless stupor. He heard Little Mary put Red John to bed. Red John was still whining 'Leave me alone, leave me alone, I'm not hurting anybody.' Then he felt Little Mary's arms about his waist and her lips to his cheek. 'My darling,' she kept saying, as she pressed him to her bosom.

Summer

1

INVERARA lay in the bosom of the sea, like a maiden
sleeping in the arms of her lover. As the sun rose each
morning, the night mists rolled away before it to the
West in pale blue columns. They rolled up the steep
slope of Coillnamhan Fort, and then banked along the
high ridge that runs athwart Inverara from south to
north between Rooruck and Coillnamhan. They lay
there at dawn, a pale blue wall dividing the east from
the west. Then the sun rose clear above the Head of
Crom, and they vanished into space as it shone
through them.

A million rays then danced on every crag. The tall
clover grass in the fields beneath the crags sparkled,
each blade an emerald. The roof of the old church at
Coillnamhan could be seen for miles, a pool of light lit
up by the sun. The trees behind O'Daly's cottage were
in bloom, an oasis in a treeless desert. Each tilled field
was big with crops. The dark green potato stalks were
covered with pink and white and red blossoms, and
tall poppies and sunflowers waved above the stalks,

scattered here and there like soldiers on sentry. Each glen along the south of Inverara was a flower garden. Sheltered by the ivy-covered hills where the sparrows chirped, the valleys were covered with pure simple little flowers, primroses, bluebells, daisies and buttercups. On the cliff-tops over the sea, where the salt air smelt like an elixir from a fairy-land, other flowers grew, whose names nobody knew. They were tender little flowers; they grew in a night and died in a day. They were as delicate to the touch as a butterfly's wing, and as multi-coloured as a rockbird's egg. Down in the crevices among the crags, where the wind never came and where the sun was only reflected by slanting dim shadows, the maidenhair ferns grew from the black earth. Their roots were moistened by water from the very heart of Inverara. Their green heads stood silent and beautiful like living poems.

All over Inverara the air was heavy with sweet smells. The wind, making slow sensuous music as it drifted slowly in from the calm sea, mixed all the smells together. It blew so tenderly that the bluebells hardly waved their heads under its caress.

Around Inverara the sea lay calm and vast like a great thought. The waves rolled slowly in on the sands at Coillnamhan. They rolled sleepily, playfully making deep channels in the sand. Then they crept back again, murmuring, 'Summer, summer, summer.' There was not one speck of seaweed along the whole stretch of sand. It was clean and spotlessly white, like the seagulls that strutted about it, with their heads stuck low on their shoulders, or scratching their breasts with their beaks. The sea stretched around Inverara, its back silvered by the sun, the waves so small that they seemed to be strokes drawn by a child's finger. Beneath the cliffs on the south there was never a wave at all. The sea there was a mirror reflecting the colours of the cliffs, yellow and black and grey. Round rocks stuck from its bosom near the cliffs, and shoals of birds scurried around in it, teaching their young how to catch fish.

The sweet languorous odour of summer permeated every living thing in Inverara. The cows standing knee-deep in the brackish pools in the meadows above the beach at Coillnamhan, chewed their cud with half-closed eyes, their tails whisking at the gadflies. Horses stood in the shade of the fences, their tails to the sun, their heads drooping and a hind leg limp, dozing through the day. The men watched their crops growing. Lying in the shade, they stretched themselves languidly and said, 'Laziness is a devilish thing.'

Nowhere in Inverara had summer so changed the face of nature as at Rooruck, and nowhere was summer so beautiful. It appealed more to the mind than to the senses, because even summer's beauty was wild and fierce at Rooruck. It was the colour of a snake, with the snake's ferocity. The great broad crag that stretched west and south from the village to the sea was so uniformly grey that at a distance Red John's black sheep, licking salt from the dried shallow pools at the summit of the Hill of Fate, looked grey too. Rooruck was like the back of a giant tortoise lying in the sea. Beneath it were the tilled fields, square and oblong, and triangular patches of green potato stalks and whitening rye, surrounded by grey stone fences. While around its shores the sea swept even in summer with mighty motion. It swept in vast hollows and unbroken

smooth ridges from north to south and from south to
north with the tides. Like a great work of art, wrought
with a few strong strokes, it lay tremendous and
beautiful. It was fierce even in its languorous silence, as
if it might rise any moment without warning and lash
into a fury, like a caged lion that dreams suddenly of a
vast forest.

In Rooruck the leap from cold gritty spring into
languorous summer was the change from northern
winter to southern skies. It filled the strong with lusty
force. It made the weak melancholy. When the heat
came, and the cuckoo's spits were lying of a morning
on the green blackberry bushes and the starlings were
scurrying about with their young, Red John withdrew
more and more into himself. His outburst of passion,
the night of Bartly's wedding, seemed to have robbed
him of strength. He did not weed his crops. He left his
pony without water or grass in a bare scorched field
among the crags, until the poor animal, mad with
hunger and thirst, tried to jump the fence and broke its
neck. One of his sheep died eaten by maggots.
Donkeys broke into his rye field and trampled the
growing rye. The neighbours shook their heads and
said, 'It's that woman has brought a curse on him.
What did I tell you in the beginning?' The whole
village noticed him going about talking to himself, but
neither the Stranger nor Little Mary paid any attention
to him. Little Mary was growing irritable. She felt that
life in Rooruck was becoming unbearable to her. Every
day when she awoke she hoped that somehow the
evening would see her flying to the mainland with her
lover. The drear black crags maddened her. The
cheerless monotony of always doing the same things,

and of having her idiot husband near her, set her
nerves jangling. And instead of deliverance
approaching, it seemed to recede. For the Stranger,
with the coming of summer, seemed to be getting
cooler towards her. She saw him smile at young
peasant women in the village. When he embraced her
he did so without passion. He hardly ever stayed in the
house, but spent the day wandering around, bathing
and lying in the sun. And she would sit on a stool in
front of her door, knitting with furrowed brows,
wondering whether he had ceased to love her. Every
time she passed a young woman of the village she
would look into her face angrily, suspecting that some
one of them had taken away her lover. Her sleep
became troubled. She had weird dreams in which she
saw her lover parted from her. And she would wake
up in the middle of the night stricken with horror,
thinking herself pregnant and deserted.

Every morning she intended to talk to the Stranger
seriously, but now Red John would sit by the fire until
the Stranger went out after his breakfast. He would do
the same at dinnertime, and in the evening, when the
languorous fragrance of summer was in her blood,
Little Mary felt too overcome by her love to take her
lover to task even when he casually embraced her.
Then one morning she awoke more vexed than usual.
'I will talk to him to-day,' she said to herself, 'to-day or
never. I can't go on like this. He must take me away
from here or I will drown myself.' Red John had
already gone out when she got up. He always got up at
dawn now, since the spring tide came, and rambled
about, nobody knew where or why. But when she had
kindled the fire, and smoke began to rise in a curling

blue column from the cabin chimney, and she had gone
to the little field below the house to milk the cow, Red
John sneaked in again and sat by the fire. When she
came in, he was drinking tea from a tin mug and eating
a piece of oaten bread that crackled when he chewed it.
While she was preparing the Stranger's breakfast, she
could see him picking the crumbs from the yellow long
teeth in his upper jaw, and swallowing something in
his throat. The apple in his throat, covered with
greyish-red hair, protruded and receded over the ivory
button at the neck of his blue frieze shirt. She would
pause in the middle of the floor, passing from the table
to the dresser, and look at him with hatred. The ashy
colour of his cheeks, instead of arousing pity in her
breast, almost made her sick with disgust. She called
the Stranger to his breakfast. She heard his answering
grunt, and then the water splashing in the basin as he
washed his face. She became very excited, feeling
certain that something definite was going to happen
that day. Perhaps it was the spring tide in her blood
too. The Stranger came into the kitchen, sleepily
murmured 'Good morning' to both of them, went to
the door yawning and looked out. Then he sat down to
his breakfast. Red John was toying with one of his teeth
that was loose, moving it from side to side, with his
eyes staring vacantly at the fire, but he was saying to
himself cunningly, 'I'll spoil their little
pass-the-time-away.' At last, when the Stranger had
finished breakfast and was rising from the table, she
could contain herself no longer. She turned on her
husband furiously.

'You lazy, idle lout,' she said, 'why don't you go out
and do something? Am I to do everything in this

house? Get out and fill the watertub for the cow, before
the sun splits its sides and the lathes fall off it. Get out,
you vagabond, and weed your potatoes.'

But she stopped, shivering and miserable. Red John
had taken no notice. He was still toying with his tooth,
and the Stranger had gone out shrugging his
shoulders. Then Red John, with a foolish laugh, got up
and followed him. He leaned over the fence, watching
the Stranger going westwards towards the shore. Then
he chuckled, and taking his fishing-basket and his line
he went up the crags to the Hill of Slaughter to fish.

The Stranger had forgotten about them when he
paused at the stile leading from the end of the road to
the shore. The hot sun stood high in the heavens. The
tide was out and in front of him the broad-bladed
seaweed growing on the outer stretch of the Jagged
Reef glistened in the sun. With his foot on the stile he
swelled out his chest and drew in a deep breath. Spring
had put flesh on his bones. The hollows in his checks
had filled. They were ruddy with health after the
manner of people living in Inverara. His eyes were
clear and far-seeing. His full-grown brown beard was
glossy and smooth. The muscles of his thigh, as his foot
rested on the stile, showed big through his clothes. He
looked around him, breathing delightedly, revelling in
his good health. Then he threw his arms over his head,
uttered a low cry and jumped the stile on to the shore.
He skipped along the crags out towards the sea. He
didn't stop until he reached the wet slippery seaweed
on the Jagged Reef, and the sea swayed blue and
mysterious at his feet. He looked down into it, his eyes
wondering with a child's wonder, sleepily, as men do
when they are healthy and their minds sleep. Then

suddenly, sleepily, he began to think. His eyes stood still. His body relaxed, and he let one foot go limp like a horse resting. He felt the sun beating on every muscle of his body through his clothes, warming and loosening the joints. His lungs were full of the invigorating smell of the sea, that itself was a mixture of many smells, seaweed, salt, and spices perhaps wafted by the breeze from distant lands where the sun always shone as in summer at Rooruck. He expanded his nostrils to drink in the scent and sat down on a high saddle of rock that was already dried by the sun. He thought that he had been transported into another world where sorrow was unknown, where the brain was a clear crystal reflecting the absolute beauty of nature, where the body was a perfect organism, impervious to disease, reacting only to joy, where the voice was only capable of song and laughter, where ... And then just as suddenly his train of thought snapped like a cord that is pulled too taut. His happiness was shattered as his Black Soul began to smile scornfully at his thoughts. As soon as he tried to abandon himself to nature his cynical intellect jeered at him. He stared at the sea, listening to its languorous deep sounds that were so silent. 'What a cursed thing is intellect!' he groaned. He put his head between his hands and bit the little finger of his right hand. Intellect, not content with the present, must peer into the unfathomable future. Not content with enjoying the surface of nature or the beauty of a woman, it must look down into the depths beneath the fair surface, probing the depths with futile shafts of thought, discovering nothing, blinded by the chaos it causes and which it cannot control.

His brain became hot and wearied with these thoughts. Little binding red lights came before his closed eyes. His body twitched. It was degrading to be feeble and neurasthenic on that beach, in the presence of that cold fierce strength, that enthralling beauty! He clasped his hands together and said, 'I must do something.' Activity would banish thought.

He looked down into a round pool at his feet, that was half-filled with smooth stones and growing seaweed. He set himself to examine the forms of life that grew there, as if he were a natural-history student on an outing with his professor. Limpets clung to its sides, their serrated, pale grey shells like cones, their yellow flat faces dimly visible as the shells rose from the rock now and again. Scores of little fishes scurried hither and thither. They would stand for a moment, sniffing and wagging their tails. Then without apparent cause they would dart under a plant of seaweed with only their watching snouts visible. Soft blue fatty lumps grew on the sides of the pool near the bottom in little circular cups cut into the rock. Long threads waved from their mouths, trying to catch food. Then a crabfish tumbled along slowly from the far corner. It walked sideways and stopped now and again to roll its eyes around. The Stranger watched it half-asleep, so calm had he become watching nature. Then the crab disappeared under a stone and he began to think again.

How futile life was! Here was he, a man, with a brain capable of wonderful thought, and yet he knew nothing definite about anything. The fishes and those soft jellies and the crab clung to life just as eagerly. Men, crabs, limpets, jellies, were all the same. There was no sense or purpose in any form of life more than in another. All life was futile. Cities and books and armies

and religions were of as little importance as one of
those limpets that heaved wearily, trying to live. They
were of as much importance as the tortuous and stupid
march of the crab from one end of the pool to the other.
They were searching for something just as the crab
was. 'What was he seeking, I wonder?' he said aloud.
Bending down, he raised the stone under which the
crab had disappeared. The crab had found a mate.
They lay in a ball. They never moved when he touched
them with a sprig of seaweed. They were in a
love-swoon, careless of their lives. 'So that is love,' he
said.

Then he said 'Je-sus Christ' as he looked back at the
world from that lonely shore at Rooruck. Two crabs
lost in a love-swoon made him look at love from an
altogether different angle. He had often argued during
his university days, when he was very young and very
sure of himself, that love was purely sensual. In Irish
fashion he had argued with equal conviction at other
times that it was purely spiritual, and at other times
that it was a combination of both. Now he understood
that his arguments had been nonsensical, 'like all
argument.' He had talked like everybody else who
discusses insolulable questions, just to hear himself
talk, like a priest explaining a mystery. 'Quite so,' he
said, 'people are very fond of explaining anything they
themselves cannot understand.' He felt contemptuous
of the civilized attitude towards love. 'Conceit and
hypocrisy! Deifying a natural form of life, crucifying
men on its account, making laws to rob it of impurities,
taking it out of the natural scheme of things and
making it moral and immoral, giving it a purpose, as if
nature had a purpose! What the devil is there behind

the embrace of those crabs? And Little Mary? Was his love for her no different, or her love for him? Lascivious Summer answered, "No." "Love," said Summer seductively, "is but an expression of life, the desire to keep living, to make other things live with you, to protect you against, against, against . . ." ' And the thought faded away into emptiness as he remembered that he had heard it somewhere a very long time ago, and that it was ridiculous and meaningless. It died in a singing sound that wafted itself out of his brain, away over the sea. It ended in the back-wash of a wave that was flopping back into the sea from the edge of the Reef. He felt weak and helpless. 'Damn women,' he said, feeling it necessary to blame something tangible for his inability to reason things out to a conclusion.

He looked down again at the crabs. They were locked in an embrace. The sight did not repel him. They looked natural there. They were a part of nature. 'But damn it, I am different,' he said. 'But how? Now tell me that, how am I different?' His intellect hungered after the meaning of things. He wanted to find something tremendous and binding, whose meaning he would be afraid to question, something that he could accept blindly, like Catholics accepted the Pope. But he had nothing. Religion was too gross and puerile. Of love he had had formerly only sickly visions: and love was based on self-deceit and fear of reality. And of his life in Inverara there were only memories of his spring lust. Now summer made things look different. Little Mary appeared different. In summer one had time to examine critically. He pictured all her defects, the pimple on her neck, the repulsive softness of her lips as she lay in his arms, the stupid look in her eyes when he said something that she did not understand. And her husband Red John! Good God, she had lain with him. She had felt his tobacco-stained lips against hers. She must have done so since he was her husband. It was like loving a prostitute. Faugh! He blew out his breath and jumped to his feet.

He walked down to the brink of the Reef, gripping the seaweed with his feet. He stood on the brink looking out into the sea. The thought of suicide came to him now seriously, as the result of the hopelessness of thought. It came not from the brain, but from the heart that could not find anything to love or reverence. It permeated his whole body, without touching his brain. His brain seemed to stand aside, indifferent. Down below him the sea waited, luring him. Behind him lay the world repelling him. It appeared to be full of strange shapes, and each shape was trying to grasp him. He could not possibly escape from those shapes other than by plunging into the sea. And yet they were all illusory. That was the worst of it. If he could only catch them and argue with them he would have no fear. But they were monstrous and intangible. There was nothing real in the cavern of his experiences. Life had been a nightmare. Now, presently, when he disappeared beneath the waves, he would awake in the reality of death.

There in front was forgetfulness. He began to bend his body forward from the hips to plunge, but as soon as he tried to move, his brain became active. He straightened himself again and his toes itched with fear. 'I wonder what it is like?' he said, assuming a tragic posture. He clasped his hands across his breast and looked out wildly. His nostrils dilated: his forehead furrowed. He was seized with such a terror of the sea and of death that he could not even scream. The sea seemed to draw him down towards its bosom. He wanted to fly, but he was numb with fright. Then his anger swelled against it. It was a siren trying to lure him, an accursed siren that devoured men and ships ravenously, a ravisher that sucked into its lustful bowels toothless old hags and beautiful young women indiscriminately, a mad giant that devours its own offspring the earth. The eternal motion of it awed him. He wanted to strike it. But where could he strike it? Where was its heart? Where its bowels? Where its head? It was the same everywhere. It resisted nowhere to the touch, like a vast mass of protoplasm. It was so confident of its power that it opened every pore of its vast face, and ships, rocks and whole continents could sink into it down to its inmost depths, and yet it moved on sardonically. It always moved. It moved. It moved. It moved. 'Stop,' he cried suddenly, 'stop, sea!' He had stretched out his hands, but they fell back again by his sides, as the sea took no notice of him. And he felt particles of the salt air clinging to the insides of his lips, and an empty feeling at the roof of his mouth, caused by the hunger-inspiring smell of the sea.

Hunger drove away his anger and his desire for death. How could he die while the sea moved that way, taking no notice of him? There was nobody to take any notice of him. The world would never hear of him. Then why die if the world never heard of his death? It would be no revenge on the world. It would be different if he shot himself with a revolver in O'Connell Street in Dublin. But even then he would be forgotten in a week, especially in that city where a dog-fight is more interesting than a score of suicides or murders. Even Little Mary would forget him and embrace the next man she met who aroused her passion, just as he had seen the crabs do. Ah! There was nothing eternal but the sea. 'Ah, beautiful fierce sea,' he cried aloud, as if he were speaking to a mistress, 'you are immortal. You have real life, unchanging life.' And just as one morning in Canada when he had seen the reflection of a vast pine forest at dawn in the eastern sky, he had stood in awe, his imagination staggered, thinking that a new world had suddenly been born before his eyes, so now, looking at the sea, the meaning of life suddenly flickered across his mind. It flashed and then vanished, leaving wonder and awe behind it.

He sat down, looking at the sea. His eyes roamed out over it, from the hollows beneath him by the jagged Reef, southwards along its glistening back beneath the Hill of Fate, then westwards where it grew bluer and vaster with silvery streaks of sunlight on it, until it joined the pale rim of the sky. He looked back again to his feet. He could see tiny ridges on every patch of water, like the muscles on the body of a giant, who was doing an eternal task, for ever without purpose. 'Oh, to have strength like the sea,' he thought. 'Just to go on fearlessly until one dropped. To be ruthless. Damn conscience, honour, everything! Nothing is worth while but ruthless strength. Happiness is for the strong. I wonder did anybody ever say that?' And he jumped to his feet.

He turned his back to the sea and kicked at the seaweed that grew at his feet on the rock. A starfish skidded from his foot and fell on its back on a little bunch of yellow moss. A piece of periwinkle-shell fell on top of it, in the centre where its four legs joined. It looked so funny and helpless that he had to laugh. It was like a compass with millions of little whitish legs sticking from its surface. It lay still for a moment, stunned by the fall. Then the little legs began to bend towards the piece of periwinkle. They gripped it. Their movement was as slow and calculated as that of hired labourers working in a State factory. Then the periwinkle began to move. The little legs appeared so minute and futile that the periwinkle seemed to crawl of its own accord. The legs, like ants, were passing it from one to another. Scores of them united to move it an eighth of an inch. At last they brought it to the brink of a leg, and a hundred or so gave it a final push over the side. It lay still immediately, like a vast rock heaved on a level plain by a thousand men. Then the legs lay still again. 'Just so the Egyptians built the Pyramids,' he mused. 'Shivering, senseless life! Men, starfish, crabs, motion without purpose. But it is motion. Nothing wants to die. It is cowardly to want to die.' He pushed the starfish back into the pool with his foot and walked up the shore, elated and gloomy. For the life of him now he could not understand why he wanted to die. But of course his scheme of values had been all wrong. It was clear to him now that the only real thing in the universe was life itself, the act of living. Nothing else mattered. No particular expression of life was important, but life itself. All expressions of life were transitional and ephemeral, like the starfish fighting the periwinkle, or the embrace of the crabfish, or the building of the Pyramids, or the death of Christ, or the conquest of Gaul by Caesar. The struggle of the Greeks against the Persians at Marathon was of no more importance to life than the struggle of the starfish against the periwinkle. The expression of life was important only to the individual since . . . 'Oh, that's all rot,' he cried, snapping his fingers, just at the climax of his chain of reasoning. 'What's the matter with me? I feel fit. The sun shines. Why worry about the world? Eh? The world is all right.'

He began to swing his arms as he reached the sun-baked, flat limestone crags above the wet shore. He struck the ground fiercely with the sole of his hard rawhide shoes. It was a pleasure even to tread the earth in his exuberant joy at having conquered his melancholy and being satisfied with life again. Then he thought of Little Mary and stopped short. 'I want her,' he thought, 'but how am I going to get her? There's Red John.' A snail was crawling across a dried-up shallow pool in the crag at his feet. It left a shiny trail on the spongy black bladders that grew on the black mud at the bottom of the pool. He smiled, looking at the snail. 'Yes, to hell with the yokel,' he said, walking on. 'Why should I let a miserable peasant stand in my way? A strong man would let nothing stand in his way.' Yet Red John still troubled him. He remembered now having seen Red John look at him a few mornings ago with murder in his eyes. He had paid no heed to it at the time, but now he remembered with a shudder that it was a cunning murderous look, the look of a madman.

He was still worrying about that look when he entered the cabin. Little Mary was sitting on a stool within the door, carding wool. A little pile of carded wool lay beside her on a mat. Her hands were covered with grease, scraping the wool between the cards. The sunshine coming in the door made an oblong shadow on the floor across her lap and her bent head. Countless little particles of matter shone like a fog of silver dust through the shadow. She looked up dreamily as he entered, and dropped her cards.

'Where is Red John?' he said, speaking aloud his thoughts unintentionally.

Little Mary flushed and jumped to her feet. Wiping her hands on her apron she moved towards the hearth and beckoned to him.

'What is it?' she said excitedly. 'Have you seen him? Has anything happened to him?' She was not feeling any anxiety about Red John, but she wanted to break through the Stranger's apathy.

'Why, what on earth are you talking about, Mary?' he said anxiously, seeing the look of fear in her eyes. 'I just asked where he was casually. Why, what's troubling you?' and he put his arms about her.

Little Mary shivered, and nestled her head against his breast. 'I think he's going mad,' she said, entwining her hands in the lapels of his coat. 'I'm afraid of him.' She was not afraid of Red John at that moment, not even conscious of his existence, although she was speaking of him. But she was afraid that her lover was no longer hers, so she was trying this scheme to win him back again.

'Rot,' he said, 'he's all right. I don't notice anything the matter with him. Eh?'

'Oh, do take me away with you,' she said gently, as she darted her head backwards and looked him in the eyes. Her eyes caught his in a flash, and then they

looked over his shoulders as if she were ashamed of
having spoken. But she was watching him without
looking at him. She watched him with every muscle of
her body that touched his. She pressed against him
seductively to arouse him. And in the languorous
silence of summer about them, the beating of their
hearts sounded loud as she looked across his shoulder
and he looked over her head at the wall beyond, his
forehead wrinkled.

'Take you with me?' he said at length. 'Eh? Where
could I take you? Good Lord, you don't know what
you are talking about!' And the thought of appearing
in Dublin with a peasant woman made him shudder.

'Yes, do take me,' she said again. She purred like a
cat. She looked him straight in the eyes now. Her head
was thrown far back so that her long lashes almost
covered her eyes, and he could see the insides of her
half-open red lips. Then she uttered a low cry, and
hugged him closely, sweeping her hands slowly over
his face and shoulders, and pressing her cheek against
his neck. 'Ha, you are ashamed of me,' she whispered
in his ear, 'you think I am not good enough for you.
But I am Sir Henry Blake's daughter, do you hear? And
my grandfather was – oh, don't hurt me.'

He had suddenly held her from him, gripping her
shoulders fiercely. He crushed her shoulders, looking
into her eyes savagely. 'What do I care whose daughter
you are? You think it matters to me who you are? Do
you think I am a man like that?'

She did not reply. They stared into one another's
faces in silence, and then ...

Something mysterious happened to him. It was
different from anything that had ever happened to him

before. In fact, he had never even imagined anything like it before. He was stupefied by it. It permeated his whole being. It was as if a sweet incense were poured into the marrow of his bones, mixed with rich wine that intoxicated instantaneously. There was the result of intoxication without its impurities. There was no heaviness in the brain. It was half-asleep like a child's brain, watching the body throbbing and exulting in response to the mysterious feeling that had seized it. And that feeling, starting nowhere and ending nowhere, was so powerful that the body obeyed it without any reference to the brain.

Slowly they sank into one another's arms until their lips met. Just before his lips touched hers, he saw her upper lip arched like a bridge, with numberless veins running crookedly upwards through the red skin. Then his lips met hers, and he forgot everything. If the world stopped at that moment he would not have noticed it. He could not think if he tried. All his capacity for thought was exhausted by the intensity of his feeling. His life seemed to have met her life, and united with it in the embrace. His body did not unite with hers, but his life. He had lost his individual being. Time lost its value. The past and the future became meaningless. He had been transported into a state which, even in its duration, he could not understand, since he had lost the power of thought. So no language has been invented to describe it, that highest point in life, whence all life might be seen naked and understood. People describe the road leading up to it, full of passion and worries and craving, and the road leading down from it, full of sourness and disillusionment. But only a god could describe the

summit itself. The great, mysterious, beautiful vision of
love in its entire purity, that vanishes into oblivion
before the arms have even tired of clasping it.

Slowly their lips parted, and they returned sighing
to individual consciousness. Their eyes still met
longingly, but the dream had passed. They were again
coming down the slope. He staggered from her arms to
a stool by the wall and sat down, his head fallen on his
chest, his hands hanging limply by his sides.

'Oh God,' he muttered, 'it is the first time, what is it?'
And he smiled stupidly.

She followed him, knelt between his knees, and laid
her head on his breast. They lay that way for a long
time, until Little Mary looked up into his face with a
nervous look in her eyes. 'Will you take me away with
you?' she said. 'You must. You must. Do you hear?'
She encircled his waist with her hands, and pressed
with all her strength.

'I am your slave,' he whispered. 'I will do what you
like ... anything.'

'My darling,' she said, 'kiss me. Oh, I am so happy.'

So absorbed were the two of them, that they did not
notice the short midday shadow of a man crossing the
square of sunlight on the floor, and then halt, stooping
at a corner of the square. It was Red John who had
come noiselessly, for in summer at Rooruck there are
no noises of human feet, but shadows. He stood by the
door, his left shoulder leaning against the wall, his left
foot on the wooden threshold, the fingers of his left
hand gripping his lower lip crosswise. Then he
laughed and they jumped to their feet, terrified. It was
a demoniacal laugh and sounded empty, as if it had
come through an endless cavern, and were going

farther. Without saying a word he sat by the fire and spat into it. Then he began to snap the joints of his fingers furiously.

The Stranger's first impulse at seeing Red John was to run away, and he obeyed it. He seized his hat and rushed from the cabin.

'Where are you going, your dinner will be ready in a minute?' said Little Mary, pretending to be totally unaware of the embarrassing situation in which her husband had found them, but her words passed him by without his comprehending them. He walked hurriedly towards the cliffs, with the forlorn image of Red John before his mind snapping his fingers.

'Poor man, poor man, I have done him a grievous wrong.' It was no use saying nothing mattered, as his reason prompted. His reason suggested closing his eyes and thinking of the delirious happiness of the embrace and the beauty of Little Mary's face, when she looked at him with love in her moist eyes. The efforts of his cold reason were washed away by the flood of remorse that engulfed him. The effort merely wearied his brain, and dissolved completely the happiness that he had experienced but a few minutes before. Red John, who was so inconsequent in his strength, was now in his weakness and misery powerful. The vision of him sitting by the fire stricken, as it seemed, brought back the dull heavy feeling in his forehead that he had felt in winter. And he was afraid of that feeling. 'It serves me right,' he groaned; 'why, oh why, did I surrender to love, knowing beforehand what it was? Just a delusion. In my case a crime. Oh!'

Summer purred about him heedlessly. He reached the cliffs and lay down flat on a green hillock. A grassy plot of ground sloped down to the summit of the Hill of Fate in front of him. It ended in a broken fringe of slaty earth, and then there was a drop of two hundred feet. A short slippery stretch of rabbit-eaten grass lay between him and a headlong fall into the sea and death. He had but to close his eyes and let himself slip, down the grassy slope, then through the silent air, and he would sink into the sea and forget everything. But would it end there? ...

'Look here,' he said to himself, and upright ridges appeared in his forehead as he frowned. 'I must get out of here. Look at the mess I am in now.' His misfortunes overpowered him. They towered over him. It was as if millions of people surrounded him, yelling at him, as boys yell at a confused and encircled rabbit, like a beautiful Magdalen at the mercy of a jury of ugly respectable women. He was afraid both of life and of death. He wanted some way of escape that did not mean suffering or effort. And nature that scorned weakness or cowardice presented none. She asked none herself, coming from the frozen sleep of winter through the icy grip of spring to the languorous ease of summer. And then his weakness struck him in its entirety. He began to analyse his difficulties and they vanished. 'I have a love-affair with a peasant's wife,' he laughed, 'and I make a mountain of it. I am a great big fool, a strong healthy idler, wasting my time and . . .' But his heart revolted at this profanation of the feeling towards Little Mary, which he felt to be too sacred for mockery. Ha! It went deeper than reason. No matter how deeply he tried to bury it under a mound of jeers and arguments and abuse, it sang down there within his breast, causing his being to throb. It said, 'I am here.

You can't deny me. I defy your brain. I am nature. I am beyond your understanding. You must submit to me, or you perish. Only nature that begat me can destroy me.' And jumping to his feet he said, 'To hell with everything. I am going to enjoy myself.'

That evening he sat with Little Mary by the hearth, murmuring soft phrases, stroking her hair, making promises, telling her how beautiful she was. And sometimes, when his reason sneered, saying, 'You can't mean what you say. It is a lie, a lie. Love is a profanity. It is against common sense,' he smothered the sneers with a laugh. Sitting in front of the fire, where two sods of turf smouldered silently in their yellow ashes, he talked eloquently of their future together. He tried by the very fury of his words to overwhelm his Black Soul that sat gloomily within him saying, 'What a fool you are. It's all a lie. You'll think otherwise in a year's time, tomorrow perhaps. How are you to know that she loves you? She only wants to use you in order to get away from here. She is making a tool of you, you idiot. All women are base and deceitful.' He fancied he could see his Black Soul smirking through a fleshless skull in a cavern of his brain. But his words, coming from his heart, talked of tearing the world to pieces and refashioning it beautifully for his beloved, as beautiful as the surface of the sea in summer, with sunbeams gleaming on it. He talked, looking at the ashes, his eyes gleaming, his right hand gesticulating with the fingers outstretched like an eagle's claws, and his left hand about her waist.

With her head leaning on his shoulder Little Mary scarcely heard his words. The sound of them wafted her into her own dreams. And her dreams were of the children of her love. She cared nothing for his dreams of greatness, but as the setting for the life that was to be, the real life of love, a child from her womb, the living expression of her love for him. For her he was then but the medium of love. Her brain knew nothing of the love of civilization. She knew but the love of nature, that obeys nothing but the blind instinct to fulfil its function and shatter the tool that has achieved its purpose. And he was trying to compromise between his brain that desired to be godlike, and his heart that talked honeyed words, stolen from the god's brains, to entice a woman in the net of his desire.

In the days that followed he tried to find that compromise between his brains and his heart, that level where he could love her without regret, and he could not. Each day merged into the next languorously, and he could decide nothing. He swayed like the pendulum of a clock from love to cynicism and from cynicism to love. When Little Mary begged him to take her away he would say, 'Why rush at things? We are all right as we are for the present. Something must happen shortly. I will fix on a plan, my treasure.' And all the time he knew that the reason that he did not take her away was because she did not satisfy his reason. He could not abandon himself to her. He was perpetually doubting her. He would say, 'Her loss would make no difference to me. Therefore I don't love her. And she would never understand me.' And yet when he had her in his arms he forgot everything in his love for her. That strange feeling of humility and purity would overmaster him, so that he often fell down at her feet and wanted to worship her. But as soon as he was alone his doubts came back again, so that he was in continual torment. For days at a stretch he would lapse into silence, merely staring at her coldly when she spoke to him, all the while trying to decide what to do with her, and whether he loved her or not, and without ever being able to arrive at a decision. In fact, the more he reasoned the more intricate the problem became. It was beyond the power of reason.

He spent most of those days on the pier, at the westward end of Coillnamhan harbour, where the boatmen from the mainland were selling turf. The pier was crowded every day by peasants buying turf or carting it home or just loafing. In summer it was perhaps the most beautiful spot in Inverara, by the harbour that ran like an azure streak through the grey rocky shores to the white sandy beach, with the green valley of Coillnamhan beyond, and beyond that the grey, sun-scorched crags rising in terraces to the cliffs. He trudged down each morning along the pier, through the brown turf dust to the farthest point. There he sat among the peasants, with his legs dangling over the wall, listening to the conversation and watching the sea. And the time flew. At one moment it would be high tide, with the sea reaching to the highest step of the iron ladders that ran down the sides of the pier and licking the base of the great rock that lay half-way up the beach at the western end. The next moment, as it seemed, it would be low tide, and the base of the pier was dry, and one could see the patch of pebbles covered with yellow moss in the centre of the strand, far out. And yet six hours would have passed. The peasants would yarn and say, 'Oh, my God, is it that time.' Then they would lie down again with their backs against a heap of turf and their hats over their eyes, revelling in luxurious idleness after the fierce struggle with spring. Sometimes they would look at the Stranger curiously and say, 'They say his soul has been bought by the devil.' Another would say, 'Don't talk of him. They say he casts the Evil Eye. Did you notice Red John lately?' Yet they talked to him with that peculiar contemptuous respect that the peasants of Inverara have for strangers whom they do not understand and despise inwardly because they are different from themselves, and are not known to possess land. 'What is he, after all?' they would say behind his back. 'Why, I tell you, he is a worthless fellow. His father was a devourer of books (the peasants' nickname for a schoolmaster), and he himself, they say, is just a useless fellow. Why, he can neither sow nor fish. By the Virgin, what queer people there are in the world. By the Book, there are. There now.'

The Stranger, on the other hand, looked upon the peasants with the interest that a lazy man might take in the horseplay of a number of puppies. On the pier he was at rest, lulled to sleep by the languorous sound of everything about him, for in summer there is nothing so languorous as the sound of other people working. The turf boats came in in the morning, sails flapped, blocks creaked, anchor chains ran out, shaggy-breasted men began to swear, horses galloped, and the sea murmured dreamily. And he listened to these sounds, as if he could never again arouse himself to take an interest in life, or make an effort. While he was on the pier he could laugh cynically when he thought of Little Mary, for it is only when the mind is restless and dissatisfied that men desire love that is more than mere sexual passion. The sun and the sea and the unexciting companionship of the men about him murmured, 'Sleep, rest, dream, for ever and for ever.' Even O'Daly, who came down to the pier every day, did not arouse in him the former interest. 'He is a boring fellow,' he would think, listening to O'Daly's interminable stories. Several times he went home with O'Daly in the evening, and met Kathleen, and even she did not arouse him. She was like a stranger to him now, and he wondered what he had seen in her before to make him desire her. 'If she only had Little Mary's beauty,' he would think, as he sat talking to her, 'what a wonderful woman she would be.' And because he was indifferent to her, he talked freely to her. But strange to say it was when he was with her that he felt his love for Little Mary most. And, inspired by that feeling, he often grew enthusiastic in praise of fine feelings and a high standard of honour and clean living, those things that are so dear to the hearts of all modern Irish, in discussion. For since no single one of the three are entirely attainable, they are ideal subjects for discussion. So absorbed was he in the contemplation of his own difficulties and his love, which, however, he would not admit to himself, that he never noticed Kathleen, or the marked change in her attitude towards him. And what a change! Was it the languor of summer that caused her cheeks to flush when she heard his step approaching? What caused her to tremble when she touched him in passing? It was fear of herself, of surrendering to the passion that she had always repressed. She prayed and fasted, trying to overcome it, that love which she considered impure because it was for another being than God. And except for the slight occasional flush and the trembling, no one would have guessed that the proud cold face concealed such furious passions. Least of all the Stranger, since he no longer took any interest in her as a woman.

Then one evening he and she were alone in the sitting-room together. She sat playing her violin in the niche by the window. A blackbird was singing on a rose-bush outside as if his throat would burst. He sat near her in the black mood that music always evoked in him, listening to the intermingling of the blackbird's voice with that of the violin. 'How impossible it is to be happy,' he mused. 'Music only makes me sad. Beauty hurts me. Beauty and the sunset. Sadness grins like an ape grinning at the futility of life. And yet men find joy in music. I must indeed be mad.' And covering his head in his hands he sighed. She stopped playing. She sat waiting for him to speak to her. At that moment she knew that she could not resist the evening, the sweet scent, the desire for ... life. But he made no movement. He was thinking of himself. And at length her pride gained the mastery, and she left the room, banging the door behind her. The noise startled him, and he sat up. Then with his eyes half- closed, as if to hide his sadness, he went out by the window.

2

WHEN summer had softened the wild beauty of Inverara, so that neither the calm sea stretching about its shores, nor the breezes sweeping its crags, disturbed the peaceful silence of nature by their clamour, the eye turned by day to the majestic sun, that stood all day in the cloudless sky, and by night to the stars, that shone forth in myriads, vast star streams with constellations wheeling slowly over the night sea. Inverara was no longer a gaunt rock, whose crude strength made the mind fierce. It was a platform from which the beauty of the heavens was visible. The fathomless blue sky, dotted by clouds that looked like washed wool tossed by a smooth wind, seemed so near that men kept looking at it with narrowed eyes, as if trying to see insects moving on its face. The island seemed to lie in the sea, dreaming of the vastness of the universe.

But the silence filled Red John with horror. He had no longer anything to distract him. The crop that he had sown in spring had withered, choked by weeds. He often looked in over the fence into his potato gardens and laughed emptily, wondering what had possessed him to spend so much labour to no purpose. Then he would catch up stones from the fence and hurl them in among the weeds, saying with a chuckle, 'Ha, I'll settle you.' He found great satisfaction in being mischievous. Everybody and everything inspired hatred in him. When a man or a woman passed him he would stare at their throats and long to draw a knife across them. And his right hand would clench the cloth of his waistcoat pocket. He often spent hours at night chasing his two black sheep, until he was lathered with sweat, his eyes blazing, furiously desiring to kill them. But when they stopped in the middle of the crag panting, and each trying to hide her head under the other's belly, he would merely claw at their wool, mumbling, wondering why he had chased them. And all the while he was unable to think. And yet it was impossible for him not to try to think.

Each day the heat of the sun and the empty vastness of the blue sky urged him to inconceivable tortures of aimless thinking. 'What is this?' he would say, looking at the sky and holding his head between his hands, with the knuckles of his fingers white with the pressure. 'What is it at all, at all? My sweet Virgin, what is it?' And the blue sky eddied towards him in monotonous blue balls, advancing first slowly, then with the rapidity of thought, until everything became a blur and something commenced to sing within his skull, and the soles of his feet itched. He would then sit down and begin to tear up the grass and count the blades aloud.

He shunned all grown-up people, but he would sit among the children and play with them at marbles or making fences with mud, chattering foolishly. And sometimes, when they made fun of him, he would grin evilly and try to entice them to follow him away from the village, desiring to kill them. That was the only persistent desire, to kill somebody. He felt that desire especially at night when he lay awake, breathing heavily. His hands would grasp his own throat and crush until the gasping of his lungs filled him with terror and he listened anxiously for the beating of his heart. But he pulled out all his front teeth and found great pleasure in the pain it caused. Then he hid them in an old mug in his barn.

He only stayed in the cabin to sleep a short while at night and to eat his meals. He never spoke to either his wife or the Stranger. He never looked at them. But he twitched spasmodically, and sometimes laughed aloud suddenly. He would open his mouth and utter a loud peal that was more like a yell than a laugh, and then shut his mouth just as suddenly, with a despairing look in his eyes as if he had resigned himself to a terrible death. Both the Stranger and Little Mary knew now that he was mad, but they never spoke of it. It made each of them miserable. Each pitied Red John, and blamed the other for being the cause of his illness. Little Mary often had fits of weeping and melancholy, when she wanted to drown herself. All sorts of fancies oppressed her. Not even her love offered her any solace. Instead of appealing to the Stranger for comfort, she shrank from him. Something seemed to have arisen between them that drove them apart. It was as if the languorous silence of nature exposed them on a wild desert, and each hated the other for being the cause of the exposure. And the neighbours, seeing the state of affairs in the cabin, whispered to one another that something should be done about it. But they did nothing but whisper, for in summer at Rooruck nobody does anything but look at the vast empty sky and whisper and dream about vast things that are unfathomable.

The Stranger used to lie in his bed at night smoking and think, 'Ah, how short-lived is happiness. Now everything is lost again. The devil take it.' He felt sure now that the past few months had been a heaven of delight, untainted by the slightest sorrow, that he had been madly in love with Little Mary, and that the future had been pregnant with happiness. Now everything was changed and he blamed Little Mary for it. 'She has driven that poor man mad,' he would say to the ceiling. 'She is driving me mad too. What is going to be the end of it?' And he would wander off cataloguing all the most dreadful fates that could befall the three of them. But each night, before going to sleep, he would determine, with tears at the back of his eyes, to have an explanation with Little Mary the following morning, to get Red John to see a doctor and to go away to the mainland with Little Mary. And yet in the morning, somehow it was impossible to speak. There was the same sleepiness in the brain, the same irritation in the heart, the same silent downpouring of heat from the sun without. It was impossible to do anything with Little Mary fidgeting about, breaking a cup one morning, sweeping the dust from the floor in his face another morning, her face wet with tears another morning. And Red John always sat immovably by the hearth, twitching spasmodically and laughing at nothing.

'Ah, something terrible is going to happen,' the Stranger would say as he left the cabin. And yet, before he had gone far, he would sink into a melancholy yet comfortable torpor, where even the most dreadful prospect did not terrify him.

He no longer went to the pier at Coillnamhan. He was ashamed to meet the tourists who now crowded the pier and the beach and everywhere along the road from Kilmurrage to Rooruck. Their happy laughter (laughter of which tourists and priests alone are capable), their gay dress, made him shun them. So he said they were vulgar, and in order to be alone he went along the south to the Yellow Cliff, midway between Rooruck and Kilmurrage. It was the most deserted spot in Inverara in summer and the most beautiful because of its majestic solitude. There indeed the silence was so great, and the emptiness so vast, that one might dream of reading the meaning of the universe, staring at the sky or looking down along the faces of the sheer cliffs into the still sea.

At the summit of the Yellow Cliff was a niche cut by nature during some great storm, aeons before, into the crag in the shape of a chair without any legs. They called it Myles's chair, after a peasant who fell down from it into the sea some hundred years before. He sat on that chair for hours at a time thinking, without moving a muscle. The perfect solitude, away from everything that even suggested men and cities and civilization, made the limbs as restful as the walls of the cliff itself. Nobody passed there excepting a solitary peasant woman who daily tended her sheep on the crags, and she merely shaded her eyes with her hand to look at him and went on in silence. The cliff stretched down from his feet, bulging in the middle so that he could not see its base. A circular bay stretched eastwards, locked by sheer cliffs, and the cliffs were intersected by three rows of cavernous slits, where rock-birds and seagulls lived and other birds with long red beaks whose names he did not know.

Sitting there his fears only made him happy. A great wave of delicious sorrow rose up within his breast, and he smiled and said: 'Ha, it is worth while to be alive and be here. Just to sit here for a time and then die.' And, inspired by his sorrow with a creative frenzy, he wanted to write a great poem about the cliffs and the sea. He felt that he knew something that nobody else knew, that he was scratching at the door behind which the secret of life lay hidden. His poem would be about that, not about the secret, but about the scratching. Nobody had ever even scratched before. He was assured of that when he recalled all that had ever been written about the sea or nature or life. It appeared superficial to him. 'They never felt what I feel. I understand. I ... I ... I.'

But then what did he understand? Looking at the sea, trying to give voice to what he understood, he found that he knew nothing. There was a pain in his heart as if something moved within him, trying to come out, and yet nothing came out. It was impossible to write anything about the sea. It was too immense. It would laugh at him. He could hear it laugh. And then he would cast aside the idea of writing a great poem, saying, 'Poetry is all very well for those who do not know the sea and nature. For those like myself, who know the sea and nature, poetry is trivial nonsense.' Shrinking from everything that oppressed him, the world, Red John and Little Mary, he clung to nature, humbly, as if appealing to it for protection. He became intimate with every ledge and slit and boss and weather-stain on the cliffs, with every wave on the bay, with every rock that jutted from the water, with its red wet mane of seaweed floating around it. He even felt kinship with the fishes prowling in the depths. He believed in the existence of the mermaids and elfs and sea-horses with golden manes who were said to live in the caverns at the base of the cliffs, where the waves sounded at high tide like cargo shifting in the bowels of a ship during a storm. The tide coming in and going out was a living thing to him. He felt that he was a component part of this complex life, that he could rest in peace, that he was free from care and danger and sorrow, that even death could not touch him.

But when he left the stone chair and the shadows of evening were falling, reality pressed in on him as blinding and heavy as a dark night on a man lost in a forest. He met groups of girls walking along the cliff-tops flirting with the young men who were out fishing in their boats, calling to the girls and singing love songs at the tops of their voices, full of the joy of summer and of life. And he passed along, gloomily conscious that the only laughter of which he was capable was the harsh laughter of sorrow. A shapeless cloud gathered around his mind, and he became again conscious of the cabin and Little Mary and Red John who was mad. It seemed so insoluble and dry and parching, that problem that lay before him in the cabin. There were three lives so intricately bound together that there was no conceivable way of arranging things. And the fear that something dreadful was going to happen grew more vivid every evening. As he came within earshot of the cabin he always expected to hear the sound of wild weeping. And when he entered the dim kitchen and heard nothing in the silence he wished that he could blow it up with dynamite and finish the torture. It was terrible, waiting for he knew not what.

Then one evening, as he was coming along the cliffs wrapped in melancholy, he suddenly came upon Kathleen O'Daly, just at the foot of the slope, where the Hill of Fate dropped to the shore at Rooruck. She was sitting on a rock, reading a book, while her father lay on his belly some hundreds of yards to the west, just at the western angle of the island, shooting cormorants. She sat up when she heard his rawhide shoes swishing along the short slippery grass coming down the slope.

'Hallo,' she said. He stopped dead and saw her. She was the last person on earth that he wanted to meet just then, when he felt sure that everybody could read in his face the sordid and disgraceful story of his life in the cabin. But looking into her face for a fleeting moment as he replied to her salutation, he saw an expression in it that made him forget the cabin in a still greater horror. Her checks were flushed. The muscles of her neck, her whole body, in fact, trembled slightly. And her eyes stared steadily, softly into his without wavering. She wanted him. It flashed on his mind that she did, and for a moment he began to wonder what had he done to her to make her look at him like that. A violent repulsion seized him. He looked around as if seeking some means of escape, and he saw her father lying out on the extremity of the rock. He started perceptibly. 'Sit down,' she said slowly. He sat down, wondering what had come over her, or whether she was really Kathleen O'Daly, or whether he was suffering from a delusion. Surely she would not ... He looked at her as if to reassure himself. And just then O'Daly fired at a cormorant. They both started and stared westwards at the little column of smoke that was rising vertically on the still air. They kept looking at it in silence until it vanished. Another five minutes and more they sat without speaking. Then Kathleen suddenly flung her book on the ground and stamped on it. 'Oh, go away,' she said, without looking at him.

He walked away in silence, with his hands behind his back. 'Now everybody has deserted me,' he mumbled. 'Now I'm alone. Good God, have I a friend nowhere! Nobody wants me for myself, but to satisfy curiosity or passion or something. I am accursed.' A cold breeze was blowing from the sea, bearing with it the smell of wet seaweed. It seemed to him to be like the smell of the balm that Egyptians rubbed into dead bodies, although he was totally ignorant of what that smell was. But death seemed to be in the air, stalking in front of him. He could smell it and feel it and fear it, but he could not see it. A horrible feeling of being utterly alone and deserted on the eve of a great danger grew intensely, until it numbed his desire to live and he felt very weak. The sun was setting, and he sat on a hillock just above the village to watch it. The sun had begun to sink into the sea to the west. He could look into its red face without blinking. Then across the sea towards Inverara the sun shadow swept in a silvery streak. It touched land and became red for a moment, then blue as it reached the tilled fields, then ending on the crags in a blaze of light that was all the colours of the rainbow. Then, as if the sun made a last dying struggle to keep back the approaching night, a flood of light poured out from it, carried on myriads of bright shafts, like the bristles of a hedgehog. The whole of Inverara and of the sea, and the flanks of the mountains on the mainland, gleamed for a minute in the staggering light, and then slowly dimmed again as the light crept away westwards towards the sinking sun, and the shadows of night pursued them and the sun sank lower and lower. The air became cooler. The wind began to make dark ripples on the sea. Stars tottered out. Then the sun disappeared.

And looking at the point where it disappeared, he shuddered and thought that somebody who had been sick for a long time within his breast had died.

Autumn

1

THEY were opening the bowels of Inverara. The potato stalks, once green, flower-decked and beautiful, were withered. They crackled as the women tore them from the ridges. The men rooted up the earth avariciously with their spades to gather the fruit that had matured in its womb during the heat of summer. Rain-bleached potatoes lay in rows on the flattened ridges. There were only bristles left in the ryefields. Inverara was being stripped naked.

The horses, carrying home the crops, no longer galloped as they did in spring. They moved slowly with downcast heads, their baskets creaking on the canvas of their straddles. There was a melancholy silence in Inverara, broken only by the bleak whine of the autumn wind, chanting the death song of the year. Cattle were driven southwards each day from the parched plains to the long hill grass in the valley between the crags. The flowers were dead. And the blackberries had ripened, the enchanted fruit that were eaten by the black devils that rode on the storm of winter.

Inverara was like an old man groaning with his years and talking of death. Rain fell each day, drowning summer. The air was damp, and heavy mists hung by day and by night over the ridge of Coillnamhan. Sometimes the mists shut out the sea, and only its sad murmur could be heard, coming through the fog like the wheezing of an old man sick with pleurisy. The shore at Rooruck was strewn with offal, rotting timber, torn seaweed, heads of dogfishes, worthless refuse after the joyous debauch of summer. The broad grey crag of Rooruck shone sombrely, washed by the ceaseless rain mist. And water gushed from the crevices in the faces of the cliffs, falling with sad sounds in zigzag courses down the cliffs to the sea, as though autumn were washing Inverara. The sun shone dimly through the dun clouds on Rooruck, dimly as if it perpetually frowned. Hosts of shadows continually flitted along the Jagged Reef southwards towards the cliffs, like spirits shielding something that fled. The men working in the harvest fields often stood erect, caressing their sore backs and cursing the laggard sun, for work that was joyous in spring was now painful, and the time dragged slowly, like a dying man's breath. For time is a measure of pain.

Suddenly, through the autumn fog, a noise came to Red John's ears. It came to him in the early morning. He was sitting by the fire, waiting for Little Mary to come in from the cow with the milk. The flood tide had just made. There was a fever in the air. The sea was fermenting. The noise buzzed in his ears and he got up and left the cabin. It was as if somebody had uttered a command and he had to obey it. He walked swiftly, without thinking, quite calmly, down to the shore, just south of the Jagged Reef. He threw out his right hand in front of his face as he walked, with the fingers extended and making signs at some invisible thing in the air. His red and white gums were bared in a grin. He was amused because he had suddenly felt that he must wash his feet in the sea and that if he did not do so he would die before night. He sat by a pool of sea-water and washed his feet in it without taking off his shoes and stockings. Then he walked back again to the cabin calmly as if he had just done a daily task.

The cabin was still empty. The Stranger slept. Little Mary was at the cow. He sat by the fire and tried to sink back into his usual idiot's dreams. But he could not. Again the buzzing came into his ears and then a pain shot across from his ears to his eyes, so that he had to jump to his feet with his eyes closed and stagger around the floor, clawing the air with his hands like a man suddenly stricken with blindness. Then he opened his eyes and there was nothing the matter with them. And the buzzing had stopped. But his head was very heavy and the backs of his calves were perspiring with weakness. He began to take off his clothes, as if to relieve his body of their weight. There was, too, a peculiar irritation all over his skin. But he had ceased thinking. His head was too heavy for thought.

It was not until he had stripped himself naked that he began again to think. He shut his mouth with a snap and his whole body went stiff. Then something began to gurgle, going down from his throat to his bowels. 'Ohé, ohé,' he muttered, laughing. 'Oh, Red John, the son of Stephen, what are you doing now?' Looking down at himself, he saw the bones sticking through his hips like spear-points and his thighs as narrow as a consumptive's wrists, and he shuddered. His body suddenly appeared to him to be shrinking and falling to pieces. He kept drawing in his breath, trying to keep it together until he almost burst. And when he allowed his breath to rush out again he began to tremble violently so that he kept jumping from leg to leg as if the floor were hot. Visions now began to crowd his brain pell-mell, in chaotic disorder, until at last he seized his head between his hands and crushed it, trying to keep his brain steady. He held his breath too. Gradually the whirling within his skull ceased and he became conscious of a desire that grew greater and greater, until he had to say aloud, 'I'll kill the Stranger.' Then he was calm again.   At least he thought so himself, but his arms and his legs below the knees were totally beyond his control and kept jerking and twitching as if they had separate lives and were engaged on some mysterious occupation of their own. But his mind was calm, determined to kill the Stranger. He stood with his back to the wall behind the door of the Stranger's room, waiting until he should come out. But soon the silence and the tension of waiting drove the thought of killing the Stranger out of his brain and he wanted to run away. But it was impossible for him to run. He had lost the use of his limbs. He was seized with terror. He thought that he was hiding from the Stranger, that the Stranger was mad and was looking for him with a gun. He tried to stretch out his right foot in an effort to get to his clothes, but the foot did not move. It would not obey his will. Even his face was creased in a foolish grin, in spite of the terror in his brain. And the sweat that stood in swelling drops on his forehead looked white against the ashy greyness of his skin. He began to knock the back of his head against the wall, keeping time with the alarum clock that ticked on the dresser beside him.

The Stranger had arisen and was putting on his boots when he heard the knocking. He went to the door hurriedly and shouted: 'Why don't you stop that noise? Who is making that noise, I say?' Red John heard and tried to stop his head from banging against the wall, but could not do so. His head, too, was beyond his control. The Stranger dashed out of his room in a fury and had just begun to shout abuse when he saw Red John standing naked by the wall. He stood with wide-open mouth and staring eyes. His face got cold and then turned white. His nostrils distended. He stared into Red John's eyes and Red John stared into his.

He was not afraid of physical hurt from Red John. He was not startled by seeing him standing naked against the wall. It was not that made him horror-stricken. It was a sudden thought that flashed across his brain when he looked into Red John's insane eyes. It was the thought that there was a kinship between his own soul and that of Red John, that he himself was mad like Red John. It was like seeing a photograph of himself taken during a nightmare. Now the terrors and excitements of the past years, since the night in France when the shells falling about his ears filled his head with red demons, gathered together with a lightning rush and formed into a word that he read, horrified, 'Insanity.' 'I am insane,' he muttered. And he was seized with a frenzy that made him stiffen against the grinning idiot opposite him, who had torn this devilish secret from his breast. He raised his hands and hissed, about to grasp Red John by the throat.

Then Red John yelled and tore his jaws wide open to the utmost with his two hands, as if trying to vomit his fear in the intensity of the yell. He drew up his right leg to his buttock and struck at the wall with its sole. 'Go away,' he screamed, clawing the air, 'go away; you are going to kill me. Help me! help me! he's going to kill me!' He yelled again and was seized with a convulsive fit of trembling. His body hopped against the wall as if it were on springs. The Stranger recovered himself at the yell. His brain cleared and he drew a deep sigh of relief. His heart throbbed loudly; he had stood on the brink of a vast abyss, staggering, and had only just by accident been hurled back to sanity, by a madman's yell. Another moment and he had been tearing at Red John's throat, a madman.

Choking with the horror of his situation he ran out into the yard to draw breath. He stood for fully half a minute in the yard, breathing in gasps. Then again he remembered Red John. He must get help. 'Help, help!' he shouted. 'Red John is mad.' He listened. A peasant thrust out his head from the door of a cabin to the right. The Stranger, looking at him dazedly, noticed that his beard was the same colour exactly as his own.

'Ohé,' cried the peasant. 'What is it?'

'Red John is mad,' shouted the Stranger as if he were repeating a formula, thinking that a dark beard would suit him better. The peasant crossed himself and disappeared. The Stranger kept on shouting 'Help! Red John is mad,' until he completely forgot all about Red John and help and the peasants and everything. He was staring at the ground with a fixed stare, wondering whether primitive men had beards, or what was the origin of the beard, since it did not seem to serve any purpose and was dangerous in battle. Wrapt in his meditation, he walked into the kitchen, but stopped with a scream, as the tongs flew past him within an inch of his jaw and rattled against the open door. He fell to the ground in terror. Red John flew out over his body, carrying his clothes in his hands. He looked up to see Red John vaulting naked over the fence of the yard on to the road. There was a black patch of dirt on his left shoulder and his backbone stood out clear under his skin as his body bent in jumping. Then he disappeared around the corner, running southwards towards the crags.

The peasants, men, women and children, rushed to the cabin. The Stranger stood at the door babbling disconnectedly, describing to each as he came up how Red John stood by the wall, threw the tongs and ran out. Then when the first excitement wore off he began to notice the silence of the peasants. They stood about saying nothing, looking at him as if they suspected him of being the cause of Red John's madness. So it seemed to him, though nothing of the kind was in the minds of the peasants. They were silent and open-mouthed merely because they were trying to realize what had happened and endeavouring to derive as much satisfaction as possible from the excitement. Their crude, undeveloped intelligence, unable to understand that one of themselves had lost his reason, surrendered itself to enjoyment and fear, like women listening to a tale about pirates or malignant ghosts. And he, unable to understand that their silence was born of stupidity, thought they were accusing him and became afraid of them. Their very number awed him. He could have fawned on them for sympathy. And his mind was vexed, for even then his Black Soul seemed to stand apart, scoffing at him for his lack of courage, his lack of being able to stand alone. His Black Soul, like a dying aristocrat beset by revolutionaries whom he had oppressed, fumed scornfully, desiring to maintain his pride to the last. His heart wanted to move up close to the simple peasants and gape with them in horror at the unknown, to babble with them and gesticulate and be vulgar. He felt there was a wonderful comfort in being vulgar, in jumping off the pedestal of cold aristocratic intellectuality and plastering himself with the mud and dirt of the loud-mouthed mass. And he jumped down. A loose-limbed man, with far-seeing and tender blue eyes, stood beside him. They called him Big Dick. He turned to him and said:

'What are we to do? Hadn't we better go after him?'

The peasant spat and shrugged his shoulders.

'What is, is,' he said, 'and must be.'

'Aye,' said another, crossing himself, 'there is cure in death, so there is.'

For madness to them was a sacred thing, a mysterious manifestation of the power of the ancient gods long forgotten, but who still roamed the air and the sea malevolently playing with the people who had forsaken them for the mighty promises of the Christian heaven.

'Let what's to be done be done,' cried Big Dick; 'get yourselves ready.' And they all went away to their cabins.

The Stranger went into the cabin and sat by the fire wringing his hands. He thought this was the end of everything. He wanted to hide somewhere where no one could find him. He was stripped now of everything, of even the self-respect that his Black Soul had still kept glimmering within him. Now he had even lost his Black Soul. He was defeated. He had even lost the power of despising himself. And then through his stupor came the noise of women shouting outside. For a moment he listened carelessly, thinking that the mob were coming to lynch him for having driven Red John mad. 'Let them come,' he muttered, 'it is the end.'

But then a woman shrieked in a shrill voice, 'Little Mary, you whore, it was you drove him mad. Let us tear her eyes out, the evil one.'

He jumped up, just as Little Mary dashed into the kitchen. She staggered against the door exhausted, as if she had run a long way from death. Her light shawl, thrown over her shoulders, was torn at the edge where somebody had grasped it. Yet looking at her it seemed to him that he had never seen anything so beautiful as her eyes that looked at him startled and beseeching.

'Mary,' he gasped, and opened his arms.

'Protect me,' she cried, and staggered to him, dropping the can she held in her hand. It fell on its side and the milk from it streamed along the earthen floor under their feet as they embraced. And as soon as he felt his arms about her he lost all fear. The problem of life became suddenly simplified. She had made a demand of him that had caused some new cell in his brain to come to life. It gave him a wonderfully clean sensation, the desire to protect her.

Then the women appeared at the door, pushing one another and threatening. He rushed at them with a yell and they fled. Then he came back to Little Mary and began to console her. She sobbed without tears in his arms. They both at last felt the calmness of love without its passion, the solidarity of love. The last barrier was broken down between them, the barrier of his intellectual pride. He was in need of somebody on whom to lean for support. She needed some one to protect her. They leaned one against the other. And they looked into one another's eyes; they pledged their lives together in silence. They had found the enduring love of mutual necessity.

They left the cabin together to join in the search for Red John. The whole village had gathered for it, but even then they were still arguing as to whether a man should be sent for the police or not. Then at last Big Dick ordered a man to go to Kilmurrage for the police and they started off for the beach. The people set off after him, saying, 'In the name of God let us go,' all in as great an excitement as if they were setting out on a campaign against a desperate enemy. They advanced in a long straggling line to the shore, with the women coming behind. They talked in whispers and walked as slowly as possible, stopping now and again to look about them carefully, their faces set in a stare of respectful sympathy, but their eyes gleamed with suppressed pleasure and with intense fear and dread when anything stirred on the crags or a bird shrieked suddenly over their heads.

When they reached the shore they halted for another consultation. Several men spoke at the same time at the top of their voices, but nothing came of the talk. They seemed in fact to be debating plans for the mere purpose of dragging the affair out to the greatest possible length. Then three boys who had gone on ahead down to the rocky beach beneath the Hill of Fate came running back screaming, 'We saw him, we saw him.' They had seen Red John clothed in his shirt and his rawhide shoes going along the boulders towards the Hill of Fate. 'Ha!' they cried, 'he's making for the caves.' But nobody moved. They began to talk again and gesticulate. They were incapable of taking any action in face of the phenomenon they did not understand. Any one of them would have risked his life in the wildest storm. Yet now they were stricken with fear of Red John, whom the day before they despised as a weakling. Just as if some ancient tradition forbade them to interfere with a fellow-man who had become suddenly possessed of a strange and magical spirit. Then, still talking, they moved along to the juncture of the shore and the Hill of Fate. The shore, strewn with small boulders, stretched to the west. To the east the Hill of Fate began to rise gradually in massive layers of rock and slate. It ran southwards for about fifty yards, and then curved sharply eastwards, shooting up to a majestic summit beyond the curve. At the curve the sea lapped its base, but there was a passage eastwards across its face, about fifty feet above the sea level. Huge boulders, some of them five hundred tons weight, lay in a chaotic mass westwards of the curve in the angle of the cliff. They formed immense and tangled caverns, and the sea, running in on the flat cracked rock on which they rested, roared dismally in the dark caverns even on a calm day.

Red John had disappeared among these caverns, and the peasants stood facing them, listening to the savage murmuring of the sea among them, like the barbaric welcome of a horde of pythons to a returned fellow. The Stranger now came up with Little Mary. He had followed the crowd, drawn by the same force that was outside of himself, some instinct that forced him to join the herd in pursuit of a lost one. He had followed it mechanically, only half-conscious of what was happening, not daring to think of what was going to happen to himself and to Little Mary. And Little Mary, walking beside him, followed him without thinking, in perfect confidence that all would be well with her as long as he was there to protect her. It was as if they were rushing headlong to the summit of a ridge, unable to stop themselves, ignorant of what lay beyond, whether a deep chasm leading to death or a level plain to safety.

And then when he reached the crowd and saw them standing chattering stupidly, he underwent another change, like a man who has been a long time cooped up in a jail and is let loose on a mountain-side where the clean wind is blowing among heather and across dark lakes and through rocky passes, filling the heart with courage and the limbs with energy and the mind with daring. He came up close to them and looked at them. In their excitement and fear their ape likeness was apparent. He lost all fear of them. Their mouths were open, as if their weak minds had fled through their mouths in awe of the unexplainable. Their strong bodies were like crippled machines without a motive power. They were like wild beasts in a cage. 'Ha!' he thought, 'I am superior to them. I have a brain.' And

for the first time in his life he understood the real value
of his intellect. And immediately he took command,
without speaking. He just moved forward and they
looked at him without speaking, as if they had been
waiting all that time for him to come and give them
orders. He felt a delicious thrill at having men
suddenly look to him for guidance, to him, a wreck.
The feeling of having power over his fellows seemed to
expand him to twice his size.

He beckoned to them to follow him with a wave of
his hand, as he moved forward towards the boulders.
He was not conscious of any emotion, but elation at
having these men follow him at his command. The
power to make them move at his bidding shut out the
consciousness of everything, of Red John, of his own
position, even of Little Mary waiting behind, waiting in
dull submission for whatever fate and her lover
pleased to do for her.

The tide was coming in. The waves simmered
around the bases of the boulders in the black pools that
countless tides had worn into the rock. And along the
wide ragged reef that dipped into the deep sea afar out,
advancing and retreating waves in confused echelons
flitted endlessly, their white manes looking grey
through the rain mist that fell slantwise, westwards on
the breeze. The breeze was hardly audible. The sky
was covered with black clouds, banked in headlong
confusion, so closely that the mist seemed to be
perspiration oozing from their crushed bodies. There
was no sound but the dreary mumbling of the sea
among the boulders, the slow fall of the breakers on the
Jagged Reef to the south-west and the hoarse cackling
of a flock of seagulls who had discovered the carcase of

a sheep floating in a mat of seaweed away out to the south.

They went in among the boulders, crawling on their hands and feet. They shouted to give themselves courage. The cliff towered above them now, rising sheerer and higher as they approached the curve. The black layer of slate in the cliff face shot out through the mist, like a vast cincture around its loins. The Stranger kept in the lead until they reached the base of the cliff. Still there was no sign of Red John. 'Search the caverns,' shouted the Stranger. 'Yes, search them, you,' everybody cried to his neighbours, but nobody moved. All feared to go down into the dark abysses on that bleak misty day, with a madman prowling in their depths. The huge masses of limestone, blackened by the mist, their sides covered with limpets, looked like living monsters sprawling on top of one another, slimy monsters that had been born thousands of years before. The peasants began to shout and babble, but they did not descend.

Then somebody shouted, 'There he is. Look out!' Red John had sprung up in front of them, just by the curve in the cliff. He was running along the ledge that led eastwards. As he was about to turn out of sight he halted and looked back over his shoulder. His grey flannel shirt was torn at the back so that his spine and thighs were bare. One of his feet was clad in a rawhide shoe. The rest of him was naked, except for the strip of shirt. There was a bloody gash on his left thigh above the knee. In his right hand he held a knife. He waved the knife and his face contorted. 'Ha-a-a-aw!' he yelled. Then he turned his head and stooped to pass eastwards on the narrow ledge. The sea lay about a hundred feet beneath him. The ledge was about eight inches wide at the curve. And the belly of the cliff swelled out almost over it. But he ran along it carelessly and disappeared. 'He is going to drown himself,' whispered the peasants. They gaped and crossed themselves. The women in the rear began to weep aloud. Red John's uncle's wife threw herself flat on a boulder, with her shawl over her head, and began to chant the death dirge. The men stood in silence, looking at the Stranger. Little Mary sat on a boulder and covered her face with her hands. 'He is going to drown himself.' The Stranger, watching the spot where Red John had disappeared, heard the sentence repeated again and again, and it seemed that each repetition was a blow struck at the elation he had just experienced, of commanding men. That Red John was going to kill himself struck into his consciousness like a heinous sin remembered after an opium dream. If Red John killed himself it was because of . . . 'I'd be a murderer,' he thought. And the thought shot him forward towards the curve before he had time to judge the reason of his action. 'Where are you going?' yelled the peasants. 'You will get killed as sure as Christ was crucified,' roared another in his ear, as if he were a mile away in a storm. The Stranger brushed him aside and advanced.

He saw in front of him the narrow ledge of grey limestone, shining with moisture, as slippery as a glass floor. A fossil stuck up from a boss on the ledge just at the curve. It showed yellowishly through the mist. And above, the cliff towered with such tremendous strength that without touching it he felt its contact, thrusting him outwards. And he looked from it to the sea, that murmured fiercely beneath; he could see lines of white foam through the mist crawling about like snakes. For a moment the horror of the danger that lay in front of him, crossing that ledge, almost petrified him, just as that little yellowish figure on the ledge had been petrified. He shuddered. But his mind was firmly set on going across the ledge. He did not know why he was going across. As he took off his shoes he remembered that Red John was a very miserable fellow, utterly worthless, that his death was a matter of absolutely no importance to the world, and that he himself in cold reason was in no palpable way responsible for that death. Then why go across that ledge, to almost certain death, in a foolish attempt to save an idiotic yokel who was better dead than alive?

As he put his trousers inside his socks, lest the ends might catch in a spur of the cliff, he recalled the obvious fact that even if he were responsible for Red John's death and even if Red John were a genius and of importance to society, his death would be of no consequence, since nothing in the universe mattered but life itself, purposeless motion. It was perfectly futile to save life. It would not even be saving life. One might as well talk of saving death. Death was just as positive, more positive in fact, than life. Ha! But then death in each case was just as positive. It was as positive in his own case as in the case of Red John. Ah! but why seek it? Why seek anything? What was the use of any effort?

He finished arranging his trousers and stood up, looking in front of him at the ledge. Then through the intricate maze of his reasoning his mind again grasped in horror the reality of his position. He cast a fleeting glance at the peasants behind and he saw only the figure of Little Mary huddled on the boulder, afraid to look up, dumb and spellbound with the accumulation of horror, until even the news that her lover was going to cross the ledge only touched her brain as a needle pricks a limb that is frozen. In the moment that his eyes swept back to her and then forward to the ledge, he took in every single detail of her figure, as if his brain were lashed by terror to a speed equal to that of light. She was leaning on her right hand against a boulder. Her dark hair strayed down over her left cheek, that was towards him. He could see by the straining of her white bare throat that her eyes were shut. And her body was indistinct under the outline of her heavy cashmere shawl, as if she had crumbled up, struck by sorrow. His love for her made him so dizzy that he was unable to obey the impulse to fly back to her until it had passed, exhausted by its own force, and he was reasoning again.

He moved a step forward, gripping the slippery rock carefully with his toes. Going back would mean losing his self-respect. There was no reason for going ahead, but to go back would mean a return to his rudderless floating in a sea of ridiculous theories about life. Instinct urged him forward. Why? It was neither because of honour, morals, principles, religion, or sense of duty. It was merely instinct that said, 'Go ahead and you will feel clean. Go back and you will have to keep arguing all your life in order to prove that you are not dirty.' He took three steps in rapid succession and then swayed slightly as his right foot skidded three inches and he grasped the face of the cliff with both hands. His heart began to beat audibly, although his breath was coming regularly. Still he moved forward towards the curve.

The ledge grew narrower. He could no longer put forward his left leg that was nearest to the cliff. He had to grip the cliff and shuffle forward with his right leg in front. His spine seemed to be melting. He was afraid to look down at the sea. He shut his eyes and stood still. Suddenly the thought struck him that Red John was waiting around the curve with a knife to kill him, even if he succeeded in escaping the fall to death. Before his closed eyes the knife appeared menacing and he was unable to escape. He opened his eyes to see whether it really was there and he saw nothing but the protruding belt of slate, swelling like a black ulcer from the cliff in front of him. Fear ate at his bowels, giving him the feeling that he had not eaten for a week. 'I had better turn back,' he muttered aloud. But he made no attempt to move backwards. In fact he leaned jauntily against the cliff and took out his handkerchief to wipe his forehead, as if he were quite at his ease. And as he wiped his forehead he thought that there was no chance whatever of saving Red John and that he was bound to go back to Little Mary, as a point of honour. But just then he heard a peasant shout, 'Ah, God of the thousand battles, what a brave man!' 'Yes, I am a brave man,' he murmured, crumbling the handkerchief in a ball. He grasped the cliff again to move forward.

Stupefied with fear he lurched around the curve carelessly in three strides, that made the cliff and the sea turn a somersault three times before his eyes. He scraped his left ankle to the bone. He gashed his left temple. As he was drawing his right leg up after the third stride, it tripped over a boss of the rock and he hurtled forward, stumbling along the brink of the cliff between the earth and sea, like a willow rod blown by a sudden squall. And then as if by magic he righted himself and walked calmly on to a broad plateau, that stretched eastwards, a triangular notch cut midway into the cliff. 'Safe,' he sighed breathlessly.

He sat down on the plateau exhausted and content at having performed a feat of such daring. But in a moment he remembered Red John and he jumped to his feet again. He had come to save Red John. He looked about him. Red John was nowhere to be seen. 'I hope he is dead,' he murmured. Voices reached him from the summit of the cliff overhead. Peasants had run up the slope from the shore and were now gesticulating above the plateau, pointing to three large boulders that leaned against the cliff at the eastern edge of the plateau, just where the plateau sank into the cliff. 'Ha!' he muttered, 'there's where he is waiting for me with his knife.' He wanted to raise his hands and ask them to take him away. But he was ashamed to do so in spite of his fear. They looked upon him as a brave man. He must keep up the pretence. 'What difference does it make if I get killed by Red John? People would look upon me as a hero. Eh? And I'll have to die some day. Everybody dies. Don't they?' He began to walk towards the boulders mechanically, but his efforts at stoicism did not prevent his body from trembling and smarting. Every muscle was uttering an inarticulate whine of terror. His limbs, although thrust forward by his will, moved with the ponderous slowness of an immense engine making its first hesitating revolution. Though his will tried to force his legs to move quickly, like the legs of a determined

courageous man, the legs pretended to be exhausted
with weariness. It seemed that the knee-cap of the right
leg had jumped off and that blood was gushing from
the wound, but when he grasped the knee he found it
was a delusion. The knee was perfectly fit. But
although he knew it was perfectly fit, he let it go limp
and dragged it after him. That gave him a plausible
excuse for going slowly. And the slower he went the
more the folly of his action grew before his mind. The
fear of death grew greater. He doubted the reality of
his environment. He thought that Red John and the
peasants on the cliff-top were a delusion and that he
himself was going to commit suicide, impelled by the
consciousness of a monstrous crime. He had a fleeting
vision of things like a cliff pressing into his forehead so
close to his eyes that the atoms in its face appeared as
big as universes. But while his mind conjured with
these delusions, his body, his desire to live, were
grappling with realities. He had dropped on his belly
and was crawling sideways up to the mouth of the
cavern between the boulders, in order to see inside it
without being seen. And when his right shoulder
brushed against the slimy black boulder and he saw
the dim interior of the cavern through a corner of his
left eye, his senses became so acute that his trembling
fear left him and he experienced the kind of morbid
enthusiasm and coolness that the soldier feels when he
is about to draw the trigger from a concealed position
on an advancing enemy. 'Red John, Red John,' he
called out loudly, 'what the hell are you hiding in there
for? It's only the Stranger out here, who has come to
save you. Come out, man, and don't be making a fool

of yourself. Nobody has got anything against you. Come out.'

He listened, panting slightly, but for a moment or two he heard nothing. Then he heard something move, with the sound a duck makes walking on slippery wet flags. Then there came the sound of teeth chattering violently, and the kind of horrid mumbling a dumb man makes when in a rage. These sounds irritated without terrifying him and he struggled to a kneeling position and drew himself up to the entrance of the cavern. He stared in. His face was within three inches of Red John's.

He lay crouching on his hands and knees, spellbound. Red John crouched facing him, kneeling on his right knee, his left hand, palm downward, embedded in the yellow sea-moss that grew on the side of a tiny pool. His right hand holding the open knife was stretched in front of him, with the point of the knife resting against the face of the cliff. Large drops of water pattered from the cliff on his naked back. And through the opening at the far end of the cavern, the sea, half-hidden by the mist, loomed up like an undulating plain that is set in imaginary motion by the shadows of a winter dawn. He looked like an uncouth monster risen from the black sea. His bloodshot eyes seemed to have been thrust out from their sockets by a violent shock that had jammed their mechanism and prevented them from getting back into their natural position. And when he breathed his whole body contracted, so that the skin lay in loose wrinkles between the ribs. His mouth and throat contorted violently, as he tried to speak. And the Stranger stared at him for several moments, speechless. Then he said in a low voice, as if afraid to hear himself, 'Come on, Red John, follow me. You'll catch cold there.' And he began to edge backwards, keeping his eyes fixed on Red John's face.

But he had barely moved when Red John roared and flung himself upon him. He fell in a heap over the Stranger's shoulders and the two of them rolled out into the open plateau. The peasants watching on the cliff-top yelled. 'The knife, the knife! he'll kill him with the knife,' came a scream from a woman, as Red John tore his right hand free and lunged at the Stranger's chest. But the Stranger twisted around and struck Red John's arm with his fist. Then he closed with Red John, grasping Red John's body about the shoulders, so that he was only able to move his legs below the knees. The Stranger pressed with all his might, and Red John struck out with his feet and snapped with his teeth, trying to bite the Stranger's left ear. Then suddenly his body stiffened. He planted his heels on the rock and raised his hips, so that his body rested on his shoulders and his heels. The Stranger, fearing that he planned a fresh attack, moved and threw his legs over him in order to crush him with his weight. But as his eyes came in line with Red John's throat he drew back. The throat was shivering like the gills of a dying fish. The whole body had gone limp. The eyes were glassy. The lower jaw had dropped. Red John was dead. His heart had burst in the last effort of his madness.

2

'ON and on I wander endlessly. I am the lord of nature. I heal and kill heedlessly. I drive men to a frenzy and soothe others with the same roar of my anger. I am the

sadness of joy. I am the ferocity of beauty.' So
murmured the sea, as the Stranger, crouching astride
the stiffening corpse of Red John, held his hands aloft
to the peasants on the cliff-top and mumbled cries for
help. Then the sea seemed to take a short leap forward
and struck the cliffs noisily. Gullies of wind eddied
westwards from the Fort of Coillnamhan, whirling in
and out under the cliffs like swallows. The mist rose
before the wind and a cloud-racked sky appeared. The
sun stared through a flimsy white cloud that had just
parted in the middle. Advancing breakers buffeted by
the wind began to turn somersaults. Sea-birds, roused
by the sudden squall, soared aloft screaming. The
peasants crossed themselves and said, 'God save us, it
is the magic wind.' And the Stranger, listening to the
chorus of sounds from nature that had a few minutes
before been wrapped in mist and silence, started as he
had been awakened from a nightmare by a bugle call.
He looked at the corpse between his legs, and a sense
of the reality of life, of his surroundings, of himself,
became so vivid that it wiped out his fear of the death
of which a few moments before he had accused himself
in terror. Instead of fear of the future, of what men
would say of him or do to him, because of the death of
Red John, he experienced a feeling of anger that was
born of a sudden access of strength. Instead of maudlin
pity for the corpse beneath him, he looked upon it in
anger, meaningless anger. Whence that anger? Perhaps
it came from the sudden rush of the sea and wind to his
assistance. Perhaps the presence of death made him
lust for life. He stood up, exultantly watching Big Dick
descend the cliff on a rope to his assistance, and he
thought of nothing but his fierce desire to get to the

cliff-top and fly with Little Mary to safety. He doubted no more. The nightmares that had haunted his soul had vanished. He feared life no more. He longed for it, with its ferocity of endeavour, of suffering and of happiness. Life as he had learned to understand it in Inverara, to the sound of the sea, strong like the hailstones that pattered on the crags, like the roar of the storm wind, like the lashing of the breakers against the cliffs. Inverara had rubbed the balm of her fierce strength into his marrows. She had purified his blood with her bitter winds. She had filled his exhausted lungs with the smell of her sea. And it was at that moment, when he came face to face with the reality of death, that the reality of life assumed a meaning for him.

Big Dick reached the plateau, and advanced towards the Stranger and the corpse, the legs of his yellow oilskin trousers clashing one against the other with a shuffling sound. 'Mother of God!' he said, crossing himself, 'he's dead.' And he looked from the corpse to the Stranger with awe and fear.

They hoisted the corpse to the cliff-top and then the Stranger put the noose under his armpits and was hoisted up. As he ascended the cliff, he felt a wonderful exhilaration as if he were being raised aloft into a heaven of happiness. And for the first time since he had rounded the dangerous curve he thought of Little Mary. And with the thought of her, he felt a fiercer anger than before, like an animal whose mate is in danger. And then he felt hands about his shoulders, and he scrambled to the cliff-top into Little Mary's arms.

For half a minute they lay clasped in an embrace that made them unconscious of their surroundings, of the angry mutterings of the men, arguing with O'Daly, who had arrived just then, of the screaming of the women, of the corpse of Red John, lying ghastly and naked against a green mound; unconscious of the wind that now tore up over the cliff-top with a savage roar. Red John's uncle's wife rushed at Little Mary, screaming, 'She killed him, she's enchanted, down with her, the whore!' and the Stranger jumped to his feet, with Little Mary clinging to his waist. He had raised his arm to strike the woman, when O'Daly rushed in between them and pushed him back. 'Go, run for your lives,' he whispered; 'run.' 'Keep back there,' he shouted to the peasants, 'or I'll get every one of you shot.' And as the Stranger and Little Mary hurried away from the cliff towards the village, the men cursed and threatened them and the women gathered around the corpse, screaming and wailing the death dirge. And Red John's livid face frowned sardonically in death, as if he were conscious that he who in life was despised and persecuted were now in his death the centre of all interest.

O'Daly overtook them near the cabin. 'Hurry! Get your things and come with me,' he panted. 'You want to leave the island immediately. Be quick. I'll give you an address in Dublin ... see you right ... I'll fix up everything here ... magistrate, parish priest doesn't want a scandal ... all ... everything, d'ye see? ... all right.'

The Stranger grasped his hand and said, 'O'Daly, you're a friend indeed. I'll never forget you.'

The old man muttered an oath under his breath and shouted gruffly to hide his embarrassment. 'Come on, damn it, there's no time to waste.'

When they entered Rooruck, it was deserted like a place suddenly stricken with a plague, and the Stranger darted into the cabin to get his money and his clothes, as if every moment he had to spend in the place were a torture to him. Rushing about the cabin he started at every sight, at the bitch that lay curled carelessly on the hearth, with the wind coming down the chimney, blowing the yellow ashes about her snout, at Red John's waistcoat lying by the stool where he had dropped it, at the upturned milkcan, and the stains of the spilt milk licked dry by the dog. But when he was passing through the kitchen on his way out, dressed in his wrinkled blue suit, with a suit-case in each hand, he looked around and heaved a sigh. For it is sad to look at even hateful places for the last time. Then he rushed out and they walked away hurriedly towards Coillnamhan. 'I'll get you some clothes from my daughter's wardrobe,' O'Daly was saying to Little Mary; 'now for God's sake keep your heart up. Everything is all right. I'll see to everything. You have life in front of you.' And as they reached the brow of the hill east of Rooruck, a weird song was carried to them on the wind from the southwest. They paused and looked back. The peasants, carrying the dead body of Red John on their shoulders, were coming in a straggling procession from the cliff, the men in front, the women behind, their shawls thrown back over their shoulders, their frieze petticoats waving in the breeze against the black sky, their hair dishevelled, their voices rising and falling mournfully through the changing rush of the wind. And behind the corpse the white-haired wife of Red John's uncle staggered, rending her hair, and her voice came distinct over the din, chanting the death dirge. 'And the screech heard at dawn shall be ever in my ears, ochon, ochon ... my sorrow pierces the bowels of the sea, oh my sorrow, my sorrow . . .'

They shuddered and sped eastwards hurriedly.

3

THAT evening the Stranger and Little Mary set sail in O'Daly's yacht from Coillnamhan for the mainland. Night was falling as they scudded out under white sails. O'Daly sat at the helm and the Stranger sat with Little Mary in the prow, looking back at Inverara. Inverara was becoming an amorphous mass through the autumn mist, a black smudge on the horizon. Then it disappeared, and only spectres of white breakers arising from the deep to embrace it remained, where it sank out of sight. Farther, and only the distant mumble of the sea against its cliffs reached their ears. Then that sound died in the murmur of the wind, through the yacht's sails.

Inverara had passed out of the Stranger's life. Tears trickled down his cheeks and he pressed Little Mary's hand. Inverara, wild, fierce, beautiful, never-changing Inverara, child of the sea, had vanished.

BY THE SAME AUTHOR

Short Stories

The Pedlar's Revenge

'This valuable collection displays O'Flaherty's amazing range
from a love idyll between a wild drake and a domestic duck to
the unspeakable comedy of the appalling Patsa delivering the
contents of his golden belly under the influence of a
cataclysmic purge, from the burning of young love in that
splendid story "The Caress", to the rheumy old man sitting by
the roadside and failing to recognise in the old woman, who
pauses in passing, the warm love of his youth.' *Benedict Kiely*

'... a gallery of human emotions, embracing a clutch of huge
eccentrics, sweet and sour remembrances of distant youth and
vivid portraits of rural Ireland ...'

The Sunday Times
ISBN 0 86327 536 2

The Wilderness

All efforts to attain happiness and beauty have failed because
we have never known where God is. Outcast Henry Lawless
has retreated into the wilderness – to find him. But the fairy
glen he has chosen has its own laws, invisibly woven into the
apparent calm. Does Patrick Macanasa's tribal claim, hovering
in ever-increasing menace, hold a real threat? Is Eugene
Raverty ready to wield the club of church power against the
newcomer's startling beliefs? Or could the rebellious
sensuality of Mrs Dillon, a symptom of the changing peasant
class, devastate everything?

Stirring the conflicting desires of the glen, Lawless's search
awakes forces ancient and unknown.
ISBN 0 86327 534 6